Robert C. Rogers

Old Dorset

Chronicles of a New York Countryside

Robert C. Rogers

Old Dorset
Chronicles of a New York Countryside

ISBN/EAN: 9783337227029

Printed in Europe, USA, Canada, Australia, Japan

Cover: Foto ©Andreas Hilbeck / pixelio.de

More available books at **www.hansebooks.com**

OLD DORSET

CHRONICLES OF A NEW YORK
COUNTRY-SIDE

BY

ROBERT CAMERON ROGERS

Author of "Will o' the Wasp," "The Wind
in the Clearing," etc.

NEW YORK AND LONDON
G. P. PUTNAM'S SONS
· · · · · · · 1897

TO THE MEMORY OF JOHN DAVENPORT
OF BATH
IN THE STATE OF NEW YORK

Contents.

A Dorset Prodigal.

A Dorset Prodigal.

I.

O NE evening, in the early part of
August, some thirty years ago,
Major Cooper entered the bar-room of
the Eagle Tavern. This hostelry, the
oldest, if not the best, in Dorset, was a
favorite halting spot in the Major's
nightly orbit. Silsbee, the proprietor,
was his friend and admirer, and among
the little assemblage of gossips who
gathered at the "Eagle" with each
evening's advent, the Major was the recognized oracle; a distinction due to his
age,—he was over seventy; his title—he
had served in the army, and still wore
his brass buttons upon his waistcoat;
and the social eminence of his family in

Dorset. Beside the already mentioned attractions of the Eagle Tavern, it may be stated that Silsbee's Monongahela was the best to be obtained in the county.

It will be readily seen, therefore, that the Major, whose tastes were autocratic and epicurean, derived much comfort from his visits to the old-time tavern, whose architecture, of the order which may be styled early Southern New York, recalled to the few old residents the bygone glories of Dorset.

Few villages in Central or Southern New York were so picturesque as Dorset. It lay in a veritable cradle of hills, its broad meadows stretching to where the forest hid the steep ascent of the mountain sides. Its little river slipped clear and noisy over the pebbles, shaded on its long pilgrimage to the distant Chesapeake by overhanging branches of elm and butternut, basswood and sycamore, and many a tree or shrub of less degree, across whose

4

tangle here and there the wild grape spread its web of emerald.

Dorset was famous for its hospitality, for its pretty women, for its kitchens, for its negroes. Some of the earliest set-tlers were from Maryland and Virginia, and had brought with them so many of their slaves that the town was invested with much of that picturesqueness and local human color so prevalent in the villages south of Mason and Dixon's line. Aunts and uncles by courtesy of complexion and white wool were common in Dorset. In the early days this little town was reached only by the medium of a yellow stage, and morning and evening horns tooted gaily as six horses swung merrily along the old post-road and halted before the Eagle Tavern. Such was Dorset forty years ago.

Now, time and fortune have wrought their changes in the once remote, old-fashioned village. Many of the old families have moved away, others have

fallen upon evil days. White frame
houses, with Grecian pillars upholding
the gabled roof, under whose eves a
half-moon window gazes upon the
street, are no longer in vogue, for the
Queen Anne cottage has appeared in
the land. There are several factories
now in Dorset ; two railroads meeting
there have gained it notoriety as a
" Junction," and all day long the shriek
of whistles and snorting and clangor
of engines call out angry remonstrance
from the indignant hills.

II.

But we must return to the Major.

Return is perhaps not the word, as
one cannot ramble among the memories of old Dorset without coming
presently upon Major Cooper. He was
a repository of all that had interested
the last three generations, and though
he took to-day good-naturedly and even
glanced with tolerance at to-morrow, he

6

was plainly in the present merely as a delegate from the past.

This particular evening he was full of the importance an interesting and still fresh item of news imparts.

" Homer," said he, addressing Silsbee, whose parents had named him with that ruthless classicism once so common in many rural districts in New York State, in the nomenclature both of individuals and places; " Homer," repeated the Major, " you can reck'lect Jimmy Barton, can't you ? "

" Wal, I guess so, Major," replied Silsbee, " him 'n' I went to school together."

" What, you 'n' young Jimmy ? " questioned the Major.

" Wal, Major," laughed the other, " he aint young Jimmy no longer. He was every day of twenty when he left, an' it 's nigh twenty years sence, an' I guess we 've kep' on gettin' old 'bout even, him 'n' I."

" You 're right, you 're right," said

7

the Major. "I was thinking you were your father, I guess. Well, poor Jim has turned up."

"You don't tell me," exclaimed Homer. "I want to know."

"Fact," continued the Major. "He's down to his old nurse, Aunt Susan Tolliver's. Young Pete, her grandson, let the thing out, and he says poor Jimmy looks like a dead man. Poor boy! So long as his folks lived here I s'pose he would n't come back. He was an awful takin' boy an' they were mighty proud of him. What a voice he had! Funny, but I can reck'lect the sound of his laugh yet. Why, I 'd rather hear Jimmy Barton laugh than most people sing."

The Major paused a moment, and taking a silver tobacco box from his waistcoat pocket, opened it, helped himself to a generous mouthful and chewed for a moment meditatively. Chewing, in the Major's prime, had been as customary as smoking among the people of his acquaintance.

During this brief interlude several new-comers, who had been listening afar off, drew near. The tavern-keeper turned to one of them, a little, weazened-faced man, upon whose countenance, colored by indefatigable tippling, an expression of great curiosity was visible : " You remember Jim Barton, don't ye, Ezry ? "

" Wal, I guess I kin," replied Ezra, whose name was Spicer. " I guess I *kin ;* why him 'n' me was———"

Here the Major, with a slight frown in the direction of the adventurous Spicer, resumed the reins of the conversation. Nothing was further from the worthy gentleman's intention than to permit another to discourse upon the theme he himself had inaugurated.

" You remember Jim Barton, Seely, and you too, Balcom," he said, addressing the remainder of the group. " Well, he 's come back at last, come back to die, I guess—down to his old nurse, Susan Tolliver's." After a moment's

9

melancholy satisfaction in the exclama-
tions of surprise and commiseration following this disclosure, the Major went
on : " I was talkin' about his laugh—
clear as a bell—you reck'lect him laughin' out in meetin' at Colonel Denison's
tipsy coachman, Black Tony ? An' how
the old judge walked him out for it ?
Well, he was a limb, was Jimmy, always
up to something. He could imitate any
livin' animal or bird. Why, he used to
put his head out of the window, about
nine at night, when the town was about
ready to go to sleep, an' crow, an', my
word for it, they 'd be twenty-five old
roosters singing out revellee in five minutes. Then Jim, he 'd laugh an' go to
bed. Why, you all rek'lect that trick,
of course."

The Major paused a moment, then
resumed in a little different voice :

" Well, he went to college, an' he got
wild there, I guess. When he came
home he quarrelled with the Judge an'
got turned off. But you know it all

just as well as I do. Mrs. Barton died first, then the family lost their money, then thcy went West. The poor old Judge 's buried in Ohio somewhere. The girls are married, the old house is torn down, an' here 's poor Jim come back at the last, to die at an old nigger woman's. There 's a history for you. Here 's old Susan now," exclaimed the Major, " an' you can get the news first-hand."

III.

As he ceased speaking a negress of almost any age between sixty and eighty entered the room. She was coal-black with white hair, and was one of the few negroes in Dorset who re-membered the slave days in the North. She walked up to the counter and placed a tin pail upon it.

"Mist' Silsbee," she said, " I want 'bout a quahtah of dat pail o' wisky. I want you' porest ; hit 's fo' extu'nal app'cation.   Good evenin', Majah," she added with a dignified courtesy to that gentleman.

"Good evening, Susan," said he. "I am told that my old friend, Judge Barton's son is at your house."

The old woman's face assumed a look of mingled grief and importance. She saw herself the centre of a curious throng, and her vanity was not a little gratified.   At the same time it was evident that she felt keenly the melancholy occurrence which had given her this present prominence.   She addressed herself to the Major, as he represented to her mind the only element in the little group to be deferred to.

"Oh, fo' de Lord's sake, yes, Majah," she exclaimed, lifting her hands and letting them fall with the gesture of one who scarcely hopes to recover from some great and recent shock—"Mast' Jim 's come back, you see"—after a short pause, during which the Major had asked for the particulars of the event, "My gal Flora's boy, he sez to me to-day, sez he, 'Gramma,' sez he, 'I seen a tramp 'sleep in de ole Barton lot, down in de cem'tery,' sez he. 'Wal,' sez I, 'I can't help dat,' sez I ; 'you run 'long now ; I aint got no time fo' you.' Wal, dis evenin',"—the old woman paused a moment and permitted her hearers' interest to intensify—"dis evenin', 'bout six, Pete, dat's Flora's boy, cum runnin' to me an' sez, 'Gramma, dat tramp I seen dis maw'n' jist gone inter de ketchin.' I went to the do' an' open it, an' sure 'nough dere he stan', eating de succotash he'd tuk off de stove like he was stahvin. I was jess 'bout to call out wen he turn an' see me, an' kin' o' laugh an' say, 'you mak' de succotash de same old way, Aunty Sue!' Lord, I did 'n' know yet who de man was, an' den he walked towahd me and sez he, 'Aunt Susan, doan you know me?'—an' den I see hit was Mast' Jim.

"But, oh Lord! Majah," cried the old woman, breaking into as ob, "hit wa' n't

de same ole han'some Mast' Jim what
we all knowed. He was pore, an' white,
an' his ha'r was half gray, an' his clo's
like a sure 'nough tramp's. An' he
look like de wind blow him away. I
sat down an' fah'ly cried. 'Oh, Mast'
Jim,' sez I, 'whar you come from, whar
you been? I's mighty glad to see you,
I is, but you look so pore an' sick, fo'
de Lord's sake, Mast' Jimmy!' Den he
come clost up to me, an' sez he: 'Aunty,
I's from most ev'rywhar' an' I 'se ben
goin' most anywhar fo' de las fifteen
yeahs,' sez he, 'an' I got kind o' tiahed
an' cum back to see you 'n' old Dorset
agin; an' I 'm precious glad to fine you
'live, too, you deah ole niggah,' sez he;
an' den he stoop an' kiss me. 'You 's
de fust woman I 've kissed in a long
time, Aunty,' sez he, 'an' I guess you 's
like to be de last I evah *will* kiss;' an'
den he fah'ly break down an' cry, an'
laugh, an' cough, 'till he most die o'
chokin'.''

Aunt Susan stopped a few moments

and wept quietly into a corner of her old plaid shawl. The group of listeners were silent. Silsbee concealed two misty eyes by appearing to be busy with something under the counter. The tears were coursing freely down the Major's withered face; Balcom and Seely were gazing with dimmed vision and ill-assumed indifference at the floor, while old Ezra Spicer was sobbing audibly.

No one seemed to care to speak first, and presently the old negress continued: "I got him supper an' put him to bed, an' he kin' o' chippered up a little an' ask 'bout all his ole frens. I say, 'you people 's gone West, Mast' Jim,' and he say he know it. And den he say slowly: 'Not all, dey is n't Aunty; I ben to de cem'tery to-day,' sez he. Den he stop. In a minute he say an' kin o' choke up: 'Mother tole me she gwine to wait fo' me heah,' sez he, 'an' she 's kep' her word,' sez he. After a while he ask whar 's his cousin John Denison, an' I say, killed in de wah ; an' he say, he was in de wah too. An' he say 'whar 's 'Lizabeth Taylor ;' an' I sez, 'why Mast' Jim,' sez I, 'she ben Missus dis fifteen yeah.' 'Missus who?' sez he. Why, 'Mis' Thorne Cooper,' sez I; an' den he say to hisself like, 'den hit *must* 'a ben her little girl I see dis maw'n.' Aftah dat he keep still a minute and den he say, 'Aunt Susan kin you git me something fo' to rub my chest wiv? I aint got no money,' sez he, 'but yere 's my ole silvah watch I done carry fo' thirty yeah,' sez he. But Susan aint askin' no money to look out fo' old Mis' Barton's chil'en, so bimeby he laugh an' say, 'Wal Aunty,' sez he, 'when I get froo wiv dis yere, you give it to Pete,' sez he, 'an' tell him look out he doan waste de time like I did,' says he. And bimeby he say he was sleepy an' tu'n on his side, an' I come fo' dis yeah wisky.''

The old woman took the pail off the counter, when she had ended her re-

cital, and turned to the door, saying:
"Charge dis yere to me, Mist' Silsbee."

"No, no, no, Silsbee," exclaimed the
Major; "no, no, no, put that to me.
That's all right, Susan, an' you tell
Jimmy I'll be in to see him in the
morning."

"And you tell Jimmy fer me, Mis'
Tolliver," added old Spicer, following
the negress to the door, "that I'll be
round to-morrow, too, an' if he wants
anything I'll—I'll borrow it fer him."
Ezra had ended with an anti-climax, for
the poor old toper, soft-hearted as a
woman, had a credit founded upon
sand.

The others had adjourned to the bar,
and were about to indulge solemnly in
a round of Monongahela. Ezra watched
them from the door. No one noticed
him apparently nor invited him to be a
party to the libations, and his last nickel
had left his society earlier in the evening. But the old man hardly felt the
oversight or regretted his impecuniosity.

2   17

His face wore a meditative look, and his eyes, whose vision was usually limited by the whiskey bottle, seemed to be gazing far beyond that amber-colored fetich, beyond its worshippers, beyond the open window, the garden, the meadow, the river and the hills, away into the past.

IV.

Some time after, when the Major and his satellites had passed the tavern door to suffer eclipse in the darkness beyond, Silsbee, coming to the counter which opened into the office, noticed old Ezra Spicer asleep in his customary chair, the marks of emotion staining his weazened cheeks. It was growing late and Homer was sleepy.

"Wal, Ezry," he called, "better wake up—fust you know ole Mis' Spicer 'l be 'long lookin' fer ye with a club."

Ezra roused himself. "Crotch all hemlock," he said with a stretch and

18

a yawn combined, "ef I haint be'n dreamin.' Dremp I was fishin', at the ole fishin' hole on Colonel Denison's bank of the river—you 'n' Jimmy Barton was along, jess as yer used ter be. Kin you remember when you 'n' Jim snared that dern big mullett that would n't bite at no bait an' how Jim laughed?"

"Wal', I do," replied Homer with a grin.

"Why, of course ye do," continued Ezra. "I was goin' to call it to yer mind to-night when the Major was speakin' of Jim's laugh, but the ole Major's so dern uppity when he gets talkin'—wants to do it all. I guess we kin reck'lect poor Jimmy's ways jess 'bout as well as he kin—ef we aint so high-toned."

Homer laughed. "Why, of course, we kin. He used to train with us most the time. Guess the ole Jedge did n't like it much, nuther, but Jim wa' n't no 'ristocrat. Ye aint goin' be ye, Ezry?"

he added, gazing with a softening look
at the old man, who was walking slowly
towards the door; "ye have n't had no
night-cap yit," and he put the amber
bottle upon the counter again and pro-
duced a minature tumbler.

Ezra paused spell-bound, but timid:
"I haint no cash, Homer," he began.

"Who said ye had? Come here 'n'
have a drink," said the other gruffly.
The old tippler came up to the counter
and took his whiskey, shaking his head,
rubbing his chest, and coughing per-
functorily afterwards. Homer filled the
glass again, and again the liquor disappeared with similar concomitant phe-
nomena. When Ezra set his glass down
the second time he was evidently much
invigorated. "That fixes me," said he.
"Homer, I 'm yours truly. I wish I
could pay ye."

"I don't want no pay," growled the
other; "but don't ye forgit to drop in
to-morrow mornin' an' we 'll go see how
Jim 's a-comin' on."

V.

When the old negress reached her cottage she found the wanderer awake, and sitting upright on the bed, talking with animation to her grandson Peter, who was perched at the foot of the couch.

James Barton must at one time have been a handsome man, but now his form was bent and spare; his hair was mottled with gray, and his face thin and pinched, with the bright red spot of the consumptive upon either cheek. His eyes were blue and full of a preternatural glimmer. It was easy to see that his mind was half-wandering as he talked rapidly with the little darkey, and the old woman attempted to send the boy away, fearful of the effect of too much excitement upon the sick man. But Barton exclaimed querulously, and with all an invalid's peevishness, against her wish. He wanted to hear about the woods, and the river,

and whether the fishing was good. And
he rattled on, asking the lad a hundred questions, speaking of groves long
fallen under the axe, of fishing-holes
and swimming-pools for years disused
and forgotten. Occasionally he would
seem to be a boy again himself, and call
the little negro, "Thorne," or "Jack,"
or "Homer," or other names of his
boyhood friends.

After a while, however, he seemed to
grow weary and turned silently upon
his side. The little boy slipped from
his place and stole out of the room, and
the old negress again entered. She
offered to rub his throat and chest with
the whiskey, but he shook his head; and
presently thinking him asleep she sat
down quietly in the outer room. In a
few moments she heard the sick man
call her. She came close to the bed.

"Sit by me, Aunty, won't you?" he
said, "like you used to when I was
afraid of the dark."

"Lord bless you, chile, 'cose I'll set

by ye." She brought an old easy chair, the gift, many years before of, Mrs. Barton. "I 'll set yere, doan you fret, honey." The man laid his hot palm upon the hard black hand of his old nurse. "God bless you, Aunt Susan," said he, "I 'll be soon asleep."

Some hours passed.

The candle, burned out, was smouldering in its socket, the old woman slept noisily in her chair, and the man upon the bed was also sleeping. Suddenly he wakened with a start, and for a moment stared in a dazed manner about him. Then recollecting himself, he turned towards his old nurse. A smile stole over his face as he noticed her deep slumber, and he half raised himself upon his pillow. The window was open, and the breeze had filled the room with fragrance from a bush of late roses. The night was already lifting, and he could see far down the road, past the walls of gardens over which peered the sunflowers with their

dusky aureoled faces, just as years before, how many years he was too weak
to care to reckon, they had peered at
him, a little white-haired boy, slipping
away with his fish-pole to the river.
He could see the fringe of trees that
marked the river's course, and on beyond them the silent, wooded hill. He
could see no new buildings—the clatter
of the factories had not yet begun.
The railroad was silent—new faces were
not yet upon the street. Only his old
friends were present. The great south
hill, the trees beside the river, the sunflowers along the post-road, and by his
side, sleeping heavily in her chair, his
old black nurse.

VI.

Perhaps it was an hour later, when
a light, boyish laugh sounded through
the room. Stirring at the sound, the
aged negress half awakening, muttered
indistinctly, and at once resumed her
sleep.

She was dreaming confusedly of the past, and the laughter coming into her dream seemed a part of it. She was dreaming of an old-fashioned, white-pillared house surrounded by a garden of dahlias, hollyhocks, and sunflowers. Down the garden paths she seemed pursuing a boy with yellow hair, who continually laughed at and eluded her. Suddenly the boy was a youth, and the youth a man, and then, as the figure drifted away and was lost amid a mist of vague, uncertain visions, once more the face of the boy appeared, faintly upon the background of her dream.

When the sun, through an eastern window, flooded the room, the old woman awoke.

She leaned forward to look at the man upon the bed. His lips were half open, and the trace of a smile lingered upon his emaciated face. She took one of his hands, and, with a cry, rose to her feet, for the hand was the hand of the dead.

25

. . . .

"I heahd him laugh in his sleep," she said, that day, to Major Cooper as he stood beside the body of his old friend's son; "I heahd him laugh like he was a boy agin. 'Foh de Lord!— like he was a boy agin."

The Denison Vendue.

27

The Denison Vendue.

ONE sunny September afternoon, it was many years ago, in the fifties, a number of people were assembled in the front yard of the Denison mansion, hearkening, and occasionally yielding, to the humorous eloquence of Lemuel Edwards, the village auctioneer, as he held forth concerning the various chattels to be acquired at prodigious bargains from the Denison vendue.

The broad front door of the old mansion stood open, and, in the uncarpeted hall beyond, chairs, and tables were huddled uncomfortably together, seemingly conscious of an impending crisis, and towering above these an aged mahogany clock, unwound for many days, gazed in gloomy silence at "Time's revenges," disdaining to chronicle these supreme hours of disgrace.

In a corner, upon a sideboard, where of old stood the silver and glass of prosperity, a few nicked tea-cups and four or five long-stemmed wine-glasses, "strayed revellers," feminine and masculine, from a remote and happy period, cast their melancholy reflections into the burnished surface upon which they stood. A bedstead or two, a few books and prints, several carpets and mattresses, and a number of minor articles of household utility, littering the wide porch, completed the tale of salvage from that wreck which once was known as the Denison estate.

For Mrs. Colonel Denison, the relict of one of Dorset's earliest and most influential citizens, had finally followed her husband and children to the grave, leaving no heirs, but many creditors, and no assets but the few articles of personal property contained within the four walls of the old house.

In the white-pillared porch where of old Colonel Denison had told his stories, aired his politics and hobnobbed merrily with his cronies, the peremptory ring of the auctioneer's hammer sounded dismally, and the coarse-grained platitudes of Lemuel Edwards mocked the echoes of old-time wit and wisdom.

By four o'clock the "Vandoo" as the term was popularly pronounced among the hills of southern New York, was almost ended, and as yet but few if any of the crowd had left the sale. It was apparent that some crowning attraction was in store for them. The auctioneer was working leisurely, with a fund of humor still unexhausted.

"Here's an ice-pitcher, a real plated silver ice-pitcher—aint no spout left to it, but it's a nice pitcher,—you take me, gents? Come, Ezry, how much do *you* offer? You're great on ice-water, *you* be."

A laugh from the assemblage greeted this sally.

"S'prised ye should *know* one, when ye see it, Lemuel," retorted the individual addressed as Ezry, (whose last name was Spicer,) and again the crowd indulged in its mirth.

Ezra Spicer was one of Dorset's characters. He was a little, withered, stoop-shouldered man of sixty, whose face, ornamented by a sandy-gray chin whisker, bore the imprint of liberal principles regarding the use of ardent spirits. He had at one time occupied a position which uncompromising frankness might style that of village drunkard, but the advance of civilization had brought competition for this post in Dorset, and Ezra had profited by the levelling spirit of the age.

"Say, Lem," added Ezra, having permitted his friends to appreciate his retort. "Aint it abaout time to come down to serious bizness?"

"Come, Lem," from another of the

crowd, "no one wants that old trash, git down to work."

"Hear, hear," from a number of voices. The auctioneer yielding promptly to the popular will, thumped loudly upon the box before him, which served as a desk, and began :

" Fellow-citizens—"

"This aint 'lection time," interposed Spicer.

" Fellow-citizens," repeated Edwards, heedless of the interruption, "when Mrs. Colonel Denison departed this life she left among her personal effects an' chattels one keg of the famous brandy brought into this here county by ole Guv'nor Craig an' by him presented to Colonel John Denison, our lamented townsman."

"Speak for yourself when you say ' lamented,' Lemuel Edwards."

The auctioneer turned in surprise to-wards the speaker,—an elderly woman, though her hair was barely touched with gray, her heavy, high arching eye-

3

brows black, and her eyes clear and
steady. She was dressed in shabby
mourning, an umbrella gripped tightly
in one hand, in the other a rusty leathern bag.

Lemuel was justly indignant at the
interruption, for besides the displeasure
he felt at being checked whilst under
full headway, he resented the slur upon
the memory of a man to whom for
many acts of kindness both he and almost half of Dorset were debtors.

"I s'pose ye come in all the way from
Rileyville jest to say that, did n't ye,
Mis' Stanbro," he exclaimed with much
acerbity, "jest because ye did n't like
him, had an ole grudge mebbe, ye have
come in now to git even with a man
dead these ten years—a man me nor
half Dorset can't never pay all we
owe to him."

"Nor I can't neither," said the old
woman calmly.

"I guess ye come jest to be spite-
ful," continued the auctioneer wrath-

fully. "I see yer hosses hitched out yonder this three hours, but I haint seen ye a buyin' nothin' yet."

"Not yet you haint," replied Mrs. Stanbro.

"So I cal'clate its jest ol'-time spite what 's brought ye here, unless it 's true what I hear folks say about the widow Stanbro—gettin' a little crazy—an' ef that 's the case, why the county-house 'll kind o' have to look after ye."

"Here, that 's enough, Lemuel," said Major Cooper, a slight, gray-haired, ruddy-nosed gentleman, whose blue coat and military buttons hinted broadly at his one-time profession—"that 's enough—you leave Mrs. Stanbro alone —recollect she 's a lady—go on with what you 've got to say, but let 's get to the point."

"Hear, hear, let 's get to the pint," ejaculated Ezra Spicer, who frequently played the part of an humble corollary to the Major. "No she aint crazy,

35

neither, Balcom," he added emphatically, to the man at his right. "An' she's ben mighty good to Mis' Spicer at odd spells, too."

Here Edwards having swallowed his indignation in deference to Major Cooper resumed his address. "This here keg—it's more like a bar'l—must hold twenty gallon—was left in the cellar by ole Mis' Denison—mebbe she forgot it, mebbe she done it intentional —I guess if the old Colonel had ben the survivor ye would n't ha' found much except keg."

"I guess you would n't," said the widow Stanbro dryly.

Lemuel paused again as if to renew the battle, but apparently thought better of it. "Now," he continued, " I'm goin' to start the bids—remember it's fine old Otard DuPuy, (the pronunciation of the auctioneer was in accordance with the principles of common school English as taught in Pulteney County,) an' the best liquor in the Southern Tier. What am I offered, gentlemen?"

"I'll give ye ten cents for the keg, for firewood," said the widow contemptuously.

"Ten cents. Ten cents. I'm offered ten cents," began Edwards, holding himself under with an effort.

"Twenty-five," said Ezra Spicer, delighted that the bidding had started within the latitude of his limited finances.

"Five dollars," said the Major, lifting the contention into an atmosphere, as regarded Spicer, hopelessly remote and rarified. The Major was aware that Homer Silsbee, the proprietor of the Eagle Tavern, was prepared to go to considerable expense in order to obtain the coveted cognac, whose existence recently discovered was already well known about the village, and so was desirous of bringing on the engagement at once.

"Five dollars!" sighed the old tippler to his neighbor. "Wal' I guess I drop out—but I had one clip at it, an' that 's more 'n I looked fer."

"Yes, owin' to yer crazy friend."

"Tell ye she *aint* crazy," retorted Ezra hotly.

"Six dollars," said Silsbee.

"Seven," returned the Major.

"Eight," from Silsbee.

"Nine," said the Major.

"Ten," said the tavern-keeper. No one present save the four already mentioned had taken part in the bidding, and Spicer and the widow Stanbro seemed disposed to become mere spectators, permitting the Major and his antagonist to bear the burden of the contest. It was generally understood among the men present that should Silsbee prove victorious the famous liquor would not be relegated to the cellar of the "Eagle" untasted by the friends of its possessor. Accordingly considerable interest was evinced as the Major called out, "eleven," to which

Silsbee promptly returned "twelve." Each of them now, in his turn, lifted the bidding until Silsbee, amid much excitement, had cried, " Thirty."

There was a pause. " Thirty, thirty, thirty," vociferated the auctioneer. I 'm offered thirty dollars for the best stuff in seven counties; old cognac that kin recollect Gineral Lafayette. Major, you 've drunk it a hundred times in the Colonel's dinin'-room; you wont let it go fer thirty dollars—thirty dollars—thirty —goin' at thirty—goin'—goin'——."

" Thirty-five," said the Major, with an effort.

He could ill-afford such an outlay from his slender capital, but the temptation was too great to be withstood. He remembered the taste of that brandy. He remembered the old days when, across the mahogany in the dining-room of the Denison house, he hurled his Jacksonian Democracy into the teeth of his old whig friend, feeding at intervals the flames of his enthusiasm

with the famous Otard cognac. Why,
the thought of it made him tipsy
with the memories of three decades.
"Thirty-five," repeated the Major,
huskily. He trusted by such a sweep-
ing advance to discomfit the ambitious
Silsbee.

"Thirty-six," said the tavern-keeper,
imperturbably.

The Major's face fell. He had lost—
he realized it. It was plain to him and
to the others that Silsbee carried too
heavy an armament. "Goin' at thirty-
six, goin' at thirty-six—any one say
thirty-seven?" The auctioneer's face
wore a contented expression. It was
proper that such a trophy as the old
Denison brandy should be in the pos-
session of what was in those days
almost a municipal institution—the
village tavern. "Goin'," he continued—"goin', goin', goin'——"

"Thirty-six an' ten cents," said a
sharp, metallic voice. The bidder was
the widow Stanbro.

The crowd stared and the auctioneer paused, open mouthed. The Major, who had turned away, came quickly back.

" What was that ye bid, Mis' Stanbro?" asked Edwards at length.

" I said ' thirty-six an' ten cents.' "

" Thirty-six DOLLARS an' ten cents, reck'lect, Mis' Stanbro," said Silsbee, patronizingly.

" Don't trouble 'bout me, Homer Silsbee," said the widow tartly. " I offered ten cents for the keg alone when the biddin' begun—that 's all the thing was wuth to me—now I 'm biddin' on what it 'pears to be wuth to some of you folks."

" Forty," said Homer, sullenly, thinking by adopting the Major's tactics to silence his new opponent.

" Forty an' ten cents," returned Mrs. Stanbro promptly. " Oh, I 'm goin' to bid above you, if it takes to Christmas, young man," she added, looking triumphantly towards Silsbee.

"Did n't I tell ye she was crazy," said Balcom once more to Ezra Spicer.

"I dunno, I dunno, mebbe she be," said the individual addressed, gazing wonderingly at the old woman as she sat, her chin high in the air, her mouth set aggressively.

"Goin," began Edwards.

"Forty-five," said the tavern-keeper.

"Forty-five an' ten cents."

"Fifty," cried Silsbee, furiously— that 's all I kin pay, that 's all it 's worth to me an' more—ef you kin beat that the stuff 's yourn."

"Fifty dollars an' ten cents, what it 's wuth to you, *plus* what it 's wuth to me," said the widow, placidly. Homer plunged his hands into his breeches pockets, and turned angrily away.

"Fifty an' ten. Fifty an' ten, goin' at fifty an' ten—goin'. Edwards stopped a moment and gazed appealingly at Silsbee. The latter shook his head sulkily. "Goin' at fifty an' ten,

goin', goin', gone. Gone at fifty an'
ten. Mis' Stanbro, this is your liquor
on receipt of fifty dollars an' ten
cents."

As the tall, spare form of the widow
Stanbro took its way to the auctioneer's
desk the crowd broke into a buzz of
surprise and speculation, but the old
woman was imperturbable.

"Caleb!" she called in her shrill,
metallic voice, while she busied herself
with the leathern bag which she carried.
A lank, raw-boned farm boy sprang
from a wagon outside the gate and
hurried towards her.

"One minute," she said, and counted
out the money upon the box before
the auctioneer. "Now," she continued,
"roll that keg into the street." Caleb
obeyed her command.

"Now," she said again, turning to
the throng behind her, "if you'll all
just come down as far as the fence, I'll
show you what use I have for the fine
old Denison brandy." She turned and

43

walked towards the gate, the crowd
following. "Caleb," she said, addressing her farm hand again, "got that
sledge?" With a grin the young man
lifted a heavy hammer from the wagon.
" *Now*, stave that keg in."

But before the hammer had been
swung the Major, rushing forward, had
stayed the impending blow. "One
minute," he cried, "one minute, Mrs.
Stanbro, in the name of common
sense—why, my dear madam—you
know I would n't offend a lady, but
really this will be an awful, a shameful
waste."

"Major Cooper," began the old
woman sternly.

"But, my dear madam——."

"Did I pay you the right sum?"
said the widow, addressing Edwards.
"I guess ye did," growled the auctioneer. "Well, then, just let me be.
Caleb?"

"But, Mrs. Stanbro," persisted the
Major, "here 's Silsbee and I will give

44

you sixty dollars for it together, wont we, Silsbee? Ten more than you gave for it—only think."

" It 's an awful waste, Mis' Stanbro," put in Ezra Spicer, who with the Major and Silsbee had drawn close to the widow. " Why just think how valyble it is, medic'nally, f'r instance."

" Is this my brandy? " exclaimed the woman once more. " You, Major Cooper, *is* it? "

" Yes, Madam," said the Major, gloomily, falling back and dragging the other two with him, " I regret to say it is."

" Caleb," said the widow, shortly, " stave that keg in."

The brawny farm hand swung the sledge high in the air, then brought it down with a crash upon the head of the cask. It yielded.

" Now, turn it upon its side."

The young man did as he was ordered, and the pungent liquor plashed and rippled musically forth, mingling

with the dust of the village street and
filling the whole air about with its po-
tent fragrance. The crowd, save for
some muffled profanity from the tavern-keeper, was silent. Presently the
widow broke forth :

" I s'pose you all would like to know
why I spilt that brandy. I 'll tell you
why. You, some of you, will remember my husband, Joe. As handsome a
man an' as good a farmer as ever lived
in Pulteney County. Well, listen to
me, I won't keep you long. He was a
whig, so was Colonel Denison. He was
strong in his part of the county an'
the Colonel knew it. An' so when
Colonel Denison wanted the nomina-
tion for Congress, he asks Joe to his
house an' flatters him up an' gets his
influence. Joe was pleased an' proud,
that 's human nature, an' it was all right
till he begun to get so deep in that he
forgot his farm, till he began to drink,
an' forget his wife. And where did he
begin——"

46

The woman's eyes were flaming under her swarthy brows.

"Where did he begin his drinkin'? Right in that house there, right on that porch, there—with old Colonel Denison, an' Governor Craig, an' Homer Silsbee's father. Oh, they were in politics, that's all. That's what Joe said to me—that's why he come home smellin' of liquor; an' he told me a man would be a fool to refuse that fine old brandy of the Colonel's. That's what he said; my poor ruined Joe." The stern face of the old woman was for a moment convulsed with a spasm of emotion and tears which she was too proud to notice rolled down her face. " I hear him now, tellin' me it was only there he ever drank—an' it was such fine old brandy, an' it could n't harm him. You know it did—you know he soon drank everywhere an' anything! Why are my boys without the education that belonged to them? Why does my girl work like a drudge at the farm? You know why. The whole town of Dorset knows why. An' so I said to myself when I heard there was a keg of this stuff to sell, I 'll buy it, and I' ll stave it in, an' I 'll spill it, that liquor Colonel Denison started my poor man with; I 'll spill it, every drop of it, an' never another shall taste it for a help to ruin. An' then he thought so much of it, the old Colonel, an' look at it now, makin' mud in the village street—keep back, you!"

She addressed these last words to Ezra Spicer, who, with a pail obtained from a neighboring kitchen, had approached the keg with the evident purpose of securing a few drops of the fast-escaping fluid. "Stand back, I tell you!" She advanced upon Spicer who beat a sullen retreat. "Not a soul shall taste it," she said, and then stood motionless and silent as the cask slowly yielded its life-blood to the soil. A dog, shaggy and yellow, inserted himself inquisitively among the throng, observed the flowing brandy, cautiously sniffed at it, and retired with sneezes and a look of reproach. The crowd laughed.

"You can laugh if you like," said the old woman, suddenly; "but that dumb beast is wiser than you be. Caleb turn the keg on end—so—any left now?"

"Aint no more left, Mis' Stanbro," said the farm boy.

"Get in then an' take the reins." The young man obeyed, and the widow stepped into the wagon after him. Her face was full of stern satisfaction. A ray of humor shot suddenly across it as she noted the forlorn expression upon Spicer's face.

"The keg's mine as well as the liquor, I s'pose," she said; "you can have it, Ezry."

A few minutes later the wagon was vanishing in a cloud of dust of its own raising, and the crowd, marvelling, were dispersing in various directions. Ezra Spicer alone remained, seated upon the inverted cask, into whose butt was burned the legend, " Otard DuPuy."

"Guess Balcom was right," he soliloquized, "jest about ez crazy ez they make 'em—an' yit, an' yit, " he murmured to himself, " I kind o' wish there 'd ben some o' that partickler insanity in my fam'ly."

Madam Callander.

Madam Callander.

I.

RICHARD COOPER had always looked forward to the time when he should find himself in love, an event placed by him in his day-dreams midway in the sequence of fortune between admission to the bar and standing for the legislature.

He was ambitious and able, and his entry upon the profession was made not successfully alone, but with credit; yet two years' practice, in waiting, found him in no way nearer the second stage of his self-appointed destiny. His mind, was at times given to dreaming; and the first briefless years of his career afforded ample opportunity to lay out a varied future for himself. Somehow

he always made courtship and marriage the corner-stone of his Spanish
castle. Sometimes he went so far as to
choose a best man, and to fill the old
church with his friends; and, on one
occasion at least, to ponder upon the
fitness of a flowered waistcoat. But he
never allowed his fancy to depict the
bride. She was not even tentatively
represented by any of the daughters of
Dorset—of Dorset, too, when famous
for its pretty women. She did not yet
exist even in nebulous shape within the
scope of his mind's eye.

Had he possessed greater prospects
he might have been regarded and criticised as hard to please in the choice
of a wife, but having no claim to peculiar eligibility he was looked upon only
as a shy young man of much self-control,
evidence of the latter quality being
found in the fact that having barely
visible means of support, he did not
utterly obscure them by marrying.

He was not unattractive personally.

54

Celtic-Scotch and New England blood, a mixture not infrequent in Pulteney County, gave him a certain virile comeliness of face, and a strong, well-knit figure. Dorset believed in matrimony and he might easily have ended his single existence. Among his family a suspicion grew up that his thoughts were drifting to some remote region, beyond the county limits. " Marry your neighbors' daughters and then 'll you know what you 're getting," said his grand-aunt pointedly on several occasions. This was thought sterling advice by all who heard it, save him for whom it was meant. To him it was distinctly unpalatable. He was waiting for Destiny, and Destiny far from attending upon his wishes spun her own web, and in her own way.

One afternoon, in latter September there was unusual stir in the main street of Dorset. A coach had drawn up before the doors of the " Dorset Patriot." A yellow coach drawn by four sorrels, and surrounded by a score of horsemen, all residents of the county, from Joe Stanbro in farmer's homespun, upon a horse better used to the plow, to Judge Caldwell in sober black presiding with ill-concealed anxiety over a bay mare whose contempt of court, as sitting at the time, was unmistakable. All were friends, boon companions and clients of Colonel Callander, who had ridden out to meet him and his wife, a bride of a week, to escort them with fitting honor to Dorset.

Richard Cooper shut the book he had been reading and went to the window.

Colonel Callander was a well-known figure in Dorset, and indeed in all the "Southern Tier." Fancy a well-preserved man of fifty standing five feet and eight inches in his pumps—eyes hazel-brown and hair of the same hue. He had, too,

"A Roman nose,
And his cheek was like the rose
In the snow."

Dress him with some care in garments apt to be affected by a middle-aged bridegroom of seventy years ago, and you have the Colonel.

More attention must be given to the description of his wife.

Unfortunately, no portrait of her at the period exists, and tradition does not always deal in detail. When Dorset was still enough of the past to value the evidence of an oldest inhabitant, that dignitary—Marcus Aurelius Tolliver, one time body-servant to Colonel Callander—was wont to say of his master's second wife:

" Dey aint nevah been beauty in de town sence. You see de Kernal, an' you suah to say, ' dar 's blood—you look at Mis' Kernal an' you 'bleege to 'low dar 's beauty!'" But when the aged Tolliver was called upon for particulars, he rambled away into various by-paths of recollection, vague and ill-defined. He always ended, however, with a bit of real description—" Her ha'r had de feel ob de co'n silk, an' de colah ob de ripe husk."

It was not strange that the old negro was at a loss to describe, categorically, the beauty of Mrs. Callander. Feature by feature there was nothing far out of the ordinary. It was the harmony of all, and the charm of a perfect skin, blue eyes full of *esprit*, and a manner sometimes criticised as insincere, because of its uniform cordiality. But her hair was magnificent. She wore it massed upon her head in a great coil of gold, drawn off her brow, which was low and broad, and giving her an air of bland dignity, charmingly in contrast with her youthful looks.

.   .   .   .   .   .

She had descended from the coach at her husband's request, and stood among his friends and constituents, bowing, smiling, courtseying when some elderly man was presented, and acknowledging a flood of compliment.

Suddenly, for no accountable reason, she looked up and caught Cooper's eye as he stared at her from his window. He was gazing with so much intentness that he was not aware that his regard was too fixed in its nature. Smiling slightly, she looked away ; but presently raised her eyes towards the window again, and finding Cooper still spell-bound, turned with a slight movement of impatience towards her husband.

Cooper turned from the window, took his hat, arranged a few papers upon his table, and left his room. He went slowly from the stairs to the street. He had no wish to join the throng below. He needed no introduction to that shining, smiling woman. He did not at the time, nor till long after, realize that this was another man's wife. He had a wild desire to escape from the four walls of a house, to be by himself in the fields, in the woods—anywhere. He wanted no roof above him but the blue sky—nothing about him but the breadth of nature. He could not account for his feeling. It seemed to him as though he had seen but half the light of day before, and now it all poured into his soul.

As he passed through the group before the door, the Colonel caught sight of him. "Why, Dick, my boy," he called, " come here and give me joy,— this is my wife. Letty, this is my friend Mr. Cooper, one of our leading lawyers."

Mrs. Callander looked up at Dick who was blushing violently, partly because of her presence, partly from the Colonel's somewhat complimentary description of him. She smiled very cordially as she gave him her hand. Cooper bowed low above it. "I saw you from my office," he said awkwardly, as he released her hand. He wished to say something, and this bald statement was all that would come to him.

"I saw you too," she answered simply ; then again she smiled. Something

there seemed to be about the young man
unlike all others she had met, something
so ingenuous and intrinsically sincere
that her eyes followed him as he slipped
away through the throng. She believed
herself in love with the excellent gentleman whose wife she was. She thought
herself perfectly happy, and one of the
daughters of men to be envied, and yet
for the first time since her wedding, she
found herself thinking of marriage as a
serious matter, entailing duties, curtail-
ing liberties. She soon forgot Dick
Cooper's name, but that evening at dinner she asked her husband about him:
"that young man with light hair and
blue eyes—the lawyer."

"George Thornton, I suppose," said
the Colonel.

"No, that was not the name."

"Oh, little Dick Cooper, a very nice
boy."

For the next week Cooper did but
little upon the work he had in hand, and
indeed it did not press him. With a

well-thumbed copy of Shakespeare in his pocket he spent many hours on the river-bank under the elms and butternuts of the Denison farm. One day, prompted perhaps by recent reading of "As You Like It" he cut deep into the bark of an oak, the letters, L. C. He had half a thought of placing his own initials beside them but a moment's consideration showed him the folly and impertinence of such an act.

He saw the Colonel's bride several times during the next few weeks, at church. He found cause to loiter outside the door until she came out, and each time she recognized him and bowed with a cordiality on which, had he been a vain man, he might have congratulated himself. Once as the Colonel stopped to speak a moment to the parson, with whom at the time Cooper was talking, Mrs. Callander was left at the young man's side. His agitation, had it not become him, would have been ludicrous. But a blush

looked well upon his face and his eyes
were eloquent though his tongue was
not. Mrs. Callander "liked good eyes,"
—she told her husband that night, and
added that young Cooper had the hon-
estest pair she ever saw—" of blue that
is," she hastened to explain, for the
Colonel's were as brown as ripe chest-
nuts. A less clever woman than Mrs.
Callander might have seen compliment
in Dick's eyes, with half a glance of her
own, as she waited that day till the
Colonel completed his chat with the
parson.

"You are coming to us to-morrow
night, are n't you, Mr. Cooper?" she said
after a moment of silence that followed
the exchange of greetings.

"To the reception, Madam? Oh yes,
I shall be very glad."

"Dick," said the Colonel—he had
bade the parson good-day and rejoined
them—"come over and dine with
me; just two old people there, Madam
and I, but I 'll give you a good drop of

sherry, and the best brandy in five counties. Will you come?"

Dick looked at the Colonel, then at his wife whose face reflected the Colonel's hospitable invitation. He wanted to accept—was on the point of doing so, when he remembered it was Sunday. His people were strict in their observance of the day, with that strenuousness that came down unrelaxed from early New England.

"I—I am afraid I cannot, thank you, Colonel," he said, "I have an engagement—that is I—well, sir, they look for me home on Sundays;"—he bowed— very red and flurried—and hastened away.

"Queer little Puritan," said the Colonel, laughing.

"A very nice boy," said his wife, thoughtfully.

"Had an engagement, ha, ha, ha!" laughed Callander, "an engagement for a cold lunch at Elder Cooper's I reckon."

"Well, he said so ; he told the truth
and he did n't want to either," said
Mrs. Callander. "He's a very nice
young man."

"Hey!" said the Colonel, looking
down at her humorously—" 'Pears to
me I hear a good deal of 'nice young
man.'" She smiled fondly at him in
return, and clasped his arm a little
closer. The Colonel was not a jealous
man, and indeed had little cause to be.

Cooper never before had been in the
Callander house. When he appeared
there the night of the reception there
was a glitter of mirrors and a shimmer
of mahogany everywhere that impressed him, and made him unhappy.
He drifted from room to room trying
to appear perfectly at his ease, and at
supper found himself in a corner of the
dining-room not far from the coffee-urn
over which Mrs. Callander presided.
Do what he could, it was impossible to
keep his eyes from her, and knowing
that she noticed this and was fully

5

aware of his presence, he ransacked
his mind for some appropriate speech.
It was one of the unlovely pranks of
fortune that his post was also near
to a bowl of generous proportions
about which was gathered a knot of
merry gentlemen led thither from time
to time by their host. During one of
his advances upon the punch, the Colonel caught sight of young Cooper
silhouetted against the wall. " Here,
Dick," he said, " you look thirsty,
come, fill up—yes, one ; with me, with
me. You know,—*Sunt qui nec pocula* "
(the Colonel knew his Horace when in
convivial mood), " come, my boy." So
Dick came, and having swallowed one
cupful with his host, drank another
with Judge Caldwell, for he always
concurred with the Court.

Then he went back to his place and
less furtively than before continued to
watch his hostess as she bent above the
coffee-cups. Presently he found that
he had thought of several things to say

to her, had he the chance. In a few moments she looked across at him again. This time she laughed out-right—the laugh of an innocent and vivacious woman amused by the freaks of a boy.

"Mr. Cooper," she said, and beckoned to him. He came at once, dimly con-scious that the law of gravitation was in some way weakening its grasp upon his feet. "Was there something you wanted to say to me?" Mrs. Callander asked with a gleam of amusement upon her face. She intended to play a little with the young man, and had hit upon a question best fitted to bring the inci-dent to an untoward finish. Cooper was not versed in the coquetry of men; he did not understand it in women.

"Yes, Madam," he said with a low bow, "I wished to say that, that, you are beautiful—you are adorable."

"Mr. Cooper!" Mrs. Callander stared at him in angry surprise. She had meant to amuse herself and had been fitly rewarded. In a moment she admitted to herself that the fault lay with her, and as she looked upon the straightforward countenance of the young man she knew that intentional disrespect was impossible from him. The displeasure faded from her beautiful face:

"Mr. Cooper," she said, "I must warn you against the punch. It's a brew for men of my husband's age."

It gave her a satisfaction to bring her husband in at the close of the episode,—for she felt he had not figured in her thoughts at its beginning,—and a certain malicious pleasure in warning Cooper from the punch. She liked his quaint manner, and what he had said did not in the least offend her, coming from him. But he must not be over bold and she had rebuked him. When she looked for him again, having attended to the cups of a group of elderly beaux, he was gone.

Cooper left the Callanders without

bidding good-night to the hostess. He slept but little that night. He saw with a startling clearness the channel into which he had turned his dearest thoughts. He was thankful to the humiliation of the evening, for it took the edge from his misery, with its little acid of wounded *amour propre*.

But he knew that he could not remain in Dorset and do himself justice in his chosen profession. He had thought before of a clerkship with a well-known law firm of New York City, open to him through a kinsman, and he determined to accept it. Two days later he took coach for Albany.

II.

The third winter of Mrs. Callander's life in Dorset was an uncommonly severe one. Twenty-five years ago it was still remembered. Wolves filled the woods upon the south hill, and many sheep, in the valley below, fell victims. Early in the winter Colonel Callander was taken ill, and the malady lingered on into the spring. His young wife was all to him that could be asked. She was undoubtedly very fond of him. He was still a personable man, and in address and polish there were few in that part of the State who ranked with him. Again, his social position, his reputed wealth, his political honors, brought him a deference even in democratic Dorset that also, in a way, was accorded to his wife. So far as her nature had ever been awakened, she loved her husband, though his dignities did not render him personally less acceptable to her. Sometimes she thought of Dick Cooper, and mused with rather more than ordinary abstraction upon his impetuosity and simplicity. She regretted his absence, for she would have liked to see him occasionally, and the days were long and uneventful.

One morning in April, Death came to

the most hospitable threshold in Dorset, and like every comer was received. Colonel Callander, of whom with all his foibles it might well have been written,

> " Not a better man was found
> By the cryer on his round
> Through the town,"

was gathered not to his fathers, but sad as it reads, to his sons, all of whom, his first wife's children, had died before him. In the great white-pillared house, with only servants to keep her company, Mrs. Callander entered upon her widow-hood.

The details of the first year have no place in this chronicle. She had become "Madam" Callander to the village, in place of "Colonel Callander's second wife," for it was now certain that she would have no successor. If she had been proud of her husband's social and political eminence before his death, this pride intensified with each month of her widowhood. The Colonel,

one of the least pompous of men, would
scarce have known how to accommo-
date himself to his consort, had he
arisen from the dead, and reappeared,
at a year's end. In some quarters her
naive certainty that her husband had
been the "roof and crown of things,"
and that she was his sole legatee in the
matter of personal importance, excited
comment, amusement, and backbiting.
With most people, however, it was
taken with good nature. The Colonel
had been an excellent neighbor, his
purse-strings were never drawn tight,
and many a rough farmer whose Jacksonian democracy would have resented
condescension or patronage from another, suffered it good-naturedly from
Madam Callander. It was believed
in Dorset, that in time, the Colonel's
widow would forget his compounding
of finer clay to the extent of taking
another mate; and when Judge Hen-
shaw of a neighboring county offered
his honored name and position, and was

refused, the town felt genuine surprise.
Not long after George Thornton, of
South Tiberius, a young man of good
family and wealth met a similar denial
and Dorset entertained doubts as to the
proper balance of Madam Callander's
mind.

She made no secret of her reason for
deciding as she had. She did not gra-
tuitously express herself, but when two
matrons whose curiosity and conscience
had become hopelessly commingled,
felt it their duty to call and ask, she
spoke with candor. "Women marry,"
she said, "usually for one of three
causes: love, wealth, or position." She
neither loved the Judge nor Mr. Thornton; she was fairly well to do, and as to
position, why, with many ruffles and
rising, she was Madam Callander, and
liked the name. People, the maxim
says, "usually take you at your own
valuation," and she was taken at hers,
which was that of her deceased husband,
plus. She lived quite alone, among her

servants, and this doubtless helped her to over estimate her position in the little world in which she moved. She was finally credited with having no heart. It was simpler, after all, to believe in her incapacity to love, than that she could not be suited, or that she was satisfied with her present lot.

III.

One day in September, when the doors of the houses stood open for what wind was stirring; a very warm day—a stray dog-day as it were—Madam Callander sat upon the west porch of her mansion, reading with great inattention, for she was in no way bookish. The sun through the elms traced shifting arabesques upon the broad path to the gate, and the maples fluttered their leaves, just turning, in the occasional breeze. The great gate clicked as it swung shut, and Madam Callander looked down the walk. A young man

74

faultlessly dressed in the mode of the city, was coming towards the door. She stared a moment in surprise, then, recognizing him, rose and went on tip-toe into the house, curiously conscious of a blush that spread across her face.

.   .   .   .

Dick Cooper had returned from New York for the first time in several years. He was greatly improved personally. His place though a very subordinate one, in the office of a city lawyer of prominence, had done much for him. He considered himself, in a way, a man of the world, and wore his clothes with as much nonchalance as though they had not been his best. As he moved about the shadowy drawing-room of the Callander house, managing every few moments to pass in review of the great mirror, he felt a sense of amusement in recalling his first evening there—the fictitious elation of the latter part of the evening, and its mortifying sequel. He was full of a confidence, born of deep inexperience, that he had attained the *savoir faire* of a worldling, and was ready to meet upon her own or even a loftier footing, the woman whom absence and determined effort had not brought him to forget.

He was preening himself at the glass, adjusting his stock and collar, and admiring the fit of his coat, when in the mirrored background, he saw the form of Madam Callander. He turned, blushing to his hair, and went a step towards her. Shame at being found before the mirror, and a sudden rush of memories, made him almost speechless. She saw his discomfiture and profited by it to hide a little confusion of her own. She had intended to treat him as Madam Callander might have treated the Cooper of four years since. He had determined to meet her as one who knew the great world, and would not be condescended to. A certain quantity, as unmeasured in its varying potency as the symbol x to nth power, had been overlooked by both. There can be no doubt that the love which Cooper frankly admitted to himself, was felt in an undefined way by the woman who stood before him. She was the first to speak.

" You are a great stranger, Mr. Cooper; you are here upon a vacation, I suppose ? "

" No, Madam," replied Dick, nettled at what he considered a suggestion that he was not his own master, " I am here permanently."

" Indeed ! As a lawyer still ? "

" As a lawyer still." There was a moment's silence. Cooper felt he was being talked down to, but could not get upon a loftier footing.

" You will find many changes," said Madam Callander, noting with approval the young man's garb—" many changes."

" You have not changed," said Dick bluntly. His society-manner, which he supposed fully acquired, had deserted him, and his old directness, one of his chief charms, flashed out unguardedly. He could not have made a more fortunate speech. Compliment, even when not so sincere as this, was dear to Madam Callander.

"Ah, yes," she said, smiling graciously. "I fear I *have*, and *you* certainly have. I should know at once you were from New York. I hardly recognize you. Yes, you have surely changed."

"Not in one way, Madam," said Dick, looking her full in the face.

She may or may not have understood him. There had always been a certain magnetism between them, and it is probable she did not miss his meaning. She rose, and ringing a bell, " Will you take some refreshment, Mr. Cooper? " she asked, in her most winning manner, then with a smile of raillery, "not punch, we don't brew it here these days."

Cooper laughed and rose too, and side by side they strolled up and down the room. " I came here to-day to beg pardon," he said ; " 't is better late than never," and again they laughed. Marcus Aurelius answering the bell, noticed several things with the eye of an observer.

" Mist' Coopeh done pick up in he looks ! Mis' Kernal blushin', blushin', fo' suah ! " He saw evidences of what seemed to him an impending complication. He was devoted to his mistress and to the memory of his master, the Colonel. As he brought in—upon a salver that used to bend under the robust drink of the late Ewen Callander —the new-fashioned beverage ordered, his face wore an added shade, of gloomy apprehension. But the disapproval of Marcus Aurelius Tolliver did not pervade the atmosphere, which was charged with friendliness ; the ice was broken and for an hour the talk rattled merrily along. At last, when Cooper took his leave, it was tempered by a request that it should be but *au revoir*.

As for the widow of the late Colonel Callander, she did not understand herself. Half indignant, half pleased, she sat alone at her supper. The heavy silver which shone before her had originally belonged to the Colonel's first wife. At his second marriage it had been re-cast in a more fashionable mold and her monogram wrought upon it. She found herself, and blushed vividly at the discovery, reflecting that, in a certain event, a change of monogram would be unnecessary. And a few moments later—it seemed ominous to her—the voice of Marcus was heard, terminating in a higher key a long but suppressed conversation with the cook:

" Change de name and not de lettah,
   Change fo' wuss and not fo' bettah."

She was greatly annoyed, more perhaps at the prophecy than at what may have inspired it.

IV.

It was a curious courtship ; full of the bitter sweet to Cooper. It need not be supposed because for once Madam Callander descended from her pinnacle that she was always minded to walk the earth. Dick was compelled to avail himself of these occasions with what patience he was master of.

One of his errors at the outset was in asserting that he had seen in New York, or elsewhere, men of as much address and presence as Colonel Callander. And his anecdotes, most of them second-hand to him, of the splendor of city houses were received with inattentive disbelief, and did not advance his suit. He wished to win in his capacity of " finished " man, but he at last came to know that in his case, as always, the " real " succeeds in the end. Himself honest, direct, simple, and truthful, was the better man in the contest upon which he had entered.

6

Meantime the town looked on in wonder. It might be thought that the success of one born in Dorset and connected with its traditions, in an affair in which influential outsiders had failed, might have aroused some degree of satisfaction. But the village, like many others of its kind, had much local envy to little local pride. Many concluded that Madam Callander was a fool—others, that she was making one of Cooper. Some who had marvelled at her loyalty to her husband's name were now incensed to think she should for a moment forget it.

That she had many returns of her devotion to the Colonel's memory is certain. It was trying to know that she would have to sink, should she marry again, to plain Mrs., from her assured title of Madam. Her circumstances though straitened since her husband's death, were supplemented by her social position. A life of modest felicity with a practically briefless lawyer seemed, at times, to present an attraction decidedly tempered. Colonel Callander had a distinct charm about him, the charm of the gentleman of the old school, and of the old world, and its remembrance was often strong in his widow's mind.

Thus it happened upon several occasions when Cooper had tried to urge his suit to an understanding, that caprice and coquetry and unworthy pride stood in his path, and turned the opportunity away into the limbo of lost chances. He was not always patient under these rebuffs. Had he been even less patient he would have fared better. He was not what is known as " masterful" towards women. He had much of the old-time impracticable chivalry that submits to tyranny from a woman, whilst smarting under it.

The winter passed swiftly, and with spring came the determination to bring affairs to a crisis.

One May evening at the edge of

dusk, he crossed the little river that ran between the town and the Callander house. Before he left the bridge he stopped and looked westward up the stream at the afterglow above the hills. He had a feeling that he was approaching some turning point in his life and that these familiar sights, the willow-bordered banks, the garrulous brown riffles, the pebbly bars, these boyhood friends, were in a sort of undefined sympathy with him. Upon McRae's hill he saw the lone tree black against the fading light,—a tree that in his boyhood seemed at sunset as mysterious as the tree of the knowledge of good and evil. He stood some moments at the bridge-end, in the fading twilight. As he walked in the dusk up the path to the Callendar house, there was an earthy smell from the garden, and the earlier lilacs lent their fragrance to the air.

Madam Callander was expecting him. Some instinct, perhaps, told her that it

was a critical hour. She hastened nerv-
ously to fence herself round as she had
often done before, with constant allu-
sion to the Colonel's virtues.   She entered upon a history of the Callander
family, and proved to her own content
that the county out of which the Colonel had made his money, owed him a
debt of gratitude for enriching himself
from its broad acres.   Scarce space for
a word was given Cooper.   Only when
called upon to assent or concur did he
find opportunity of speech.   His determination, which he had resolved should
this night prevail, retired baffled.   Any
word as to a husband future seemed
out of keeping in this atmosphere of
husband past.   He was discomfited
and also incensed, and it was a burst of
temper that finally cleared the course
for plainer sailing.

"He was the first gentleman of the
county," said Madam Callander, wav-
ing her fan dreamily; "the first, and indeed the only one,—I mean," she added

hastily, for she saw the quick flash of resentment in Cooper's eye, " the only one according to old-world ways of thinking." The first part of her sentence had been enough without its ill-chosen ending.

Cooper rose.

" Madam, you and I think very differently. I believe there were a score as good, yes, and some better, than Colonel Callander ! "

" Sir ! "

" Yes, Madam, I mean it. What was he more than we? and he was no American, by birth at least."

" Ah, no, he could n't be President, as you may be, some day, could he Mr. Cooper? But he was a gentleman, and there is no one in this town worthy of being thought of in the same minute with him."

" No one ? "

" No one—that is—" Cooper was too angry to notice the tremulous look about Madam Callander's mouth, or to

86

heed the little shake in her voice. He was very proud, falsely so, in some degree. His family was as good as any in the county, better than many, aware of its respectability but bitterly conscious of its poverty as well.

He turned and went a few steps towards the door. Then he faced about and bowed low. " I wish you had told me before, Madam," he said. She had risen and come a few steps nearer him. " Why should I, pray ? " she asked in a fine tone of disdain which was far from sincere, and which did not conceal a pang of regret and alarm. The words, not the voice, touched Cooper.

" Why ? Madam, why ? Because for the last six months, day after day, I 've been hoping, believing, that at some time you, you might, as you 've sometimes acted, learn to love me."

" Mr. Cooper ! "

" Yes, Madam, you have, indeed you have ! You can't deny it."

" You are forgetting——"

"I know I am; I can't help it. Ah, Madam, Letty," he cried taking her hand which she passively left to him, "why can't you be yourself for once—for once, dearest, just once!"

Madam Callander disengaged her hand and seated herself. She was pleased with Cooper's fervor and gratified with his spirit, but she had no intention of sudden capitulation. Cooper came to her side and bent over her. "Ah, Letty!" he said, "Letty! I've loved you so long, since I first saw you—and none but you. Care for me a little, tell me you will—just a little, even! I'll do anything, everything, to be worthy of you. Can't you, dearest?"

She had been listening in a rapt, attentive way to what he said, but her eyes were fixed upon some distant object. Suddenly she sobbed and raised her hands to her face. Cooper turned hastily in the direction that her eyes had held and saw gazing benignantly from the canvas, the portrait of Colonel Callander. He looked down at her. Her face was bent forward, and her hair had fallen about her temples.

" Have I made a mistake?" he said huskily. She did not answer.

" Well," he said, after a moment, " I have forgotten myself, Madam—I wish to God I might forget you. Oh, Letty," he cried holding out his hands once more—" why can't it be, why will you not come out of your past and leave him? Let *him* be the one forgot! What right has he between us now?"

She was silent still, but was leaning a little towards him, her face bent upon her breast. He would have kissed the ground she trod upon, but he dared not, unbidden, touch her lips.

It is an old saying—about the faint heart and the fair lady—and there is a kind of restraint, half chivalric respect, half inexperience, that is at times as fatal as faint-heartedness.

There was another moment of silence, and then a sudden belief that he had been played with sprang up in Cooper's mind. "Well," he said, "I was mistaken. Good-bye." He went into the hall, took his hat, then said again, "Good-bye." There was still no answer and he went out into the darkness. The path reeled before him, his eyes were burning, but as yet undimmed; his throat seemed parched. In the shadow of the great stone gate-post he stopped, let the gate swing to again without passing it, and leaned against the wall to recover his self-command. Presently he heard footsteps, then his name called. It was Madam Callander, and in a moment she stood by the gate, opened it and ran down the dark road, "Dick! Dick!" he heard her cry. His name had never sounded so sweet to him before, and there was a ring in her voice that he had never heard till then. The light dawned upon his mind and he understood.

At first he started to follow her, then, supposing that she would return at once, he drew back. A little tingling of wounded self-pride still teased him. He had run after her, been her dog, her shadow, so long, it was not unpleasant to think of her now pursuing him, so he waited in shadow of the wall.

Some minutes passed,—hours they seemed to him. His resentment, his desire for petty revenge, had left him —showing to him as it went the un- manly thing it was. He became fearful that some harm might have come to her, when suddenly, as he was about to go in search, he heard her coming up the road. In the light of the rising moon, a light that did not yet disclose his shelter, he saw her. Her beautiful hair, " yellow like the husk of the ripe corn," had fallen about her shoulders, her hands were clasped in front of her, and she was crying unrestrainedly. As she came to the gate his impulse was to step forward, open it, and take her in

his arms. Then he felt a sense of being
an eavesdropper, one who had unfairly
surprised her in a mood he had by his
pettishness lost the right to enter. He
knew her pride and feared its workings,
should she know he had seen her in
humiliation.

She came into the yard and stood a
moment looking across the gate, the
tears bright upon her face in the moon-
light. Then she turned, so near him
he could almost touch her, shivered
slightly and went up the path to the
house. He waited until he heard the
click of the door as it swung shut,
then softly opened the gate and took
his way to the village.

That night he wrote a long and
polite letter to his friend in New
York, stating that his determination to
practice his profession in Dorset would
be final, and thanked him for his past
favors and courtesies. He also, before
closing his letter, asked that his friend
would purchase for him, repaying him-

self out of certain moneys then due and owing him from the firm, a piece of silk of flowered pattern, designed for waist-coats, one in all ways suitable to a man of thirty, contemplating matrimony. Then he sealed the letter, marked it personal, with heavy underscorings, and went to bed.

IV.

At four o'clock the following after-noon, Cooper was again upon the bridge. Half way across he saw the doctor's gig moving sedately towards him. It did not occur to Dick that the doctor's countenance as he nodded to him was grave from aught but professional cares. The great gate to the Callander place stood wide open, and as he entered the other physician of the village drove by him to the road. Then in an instant fear fell upon him and he stopped, startled and faint. He looked towards the windows of the room he knew was Madam Callander's. The shutters were closed. He went eagerly to the porch and mounted the steps. The great knocker was swathed and muffled. As he stood trembling before the well-known threshold, black Phebe came tiptoeing around a corner of the broad porch. " For God's, sake what's wrong ? " said Cooper tremulously. The woman sobbed hoarsely and came nearer. " Mis' Kernal very bad, suh," she whispered, crumpling and kneading her apron in her hands. " She done have two doctahs. Fevah, suh, typhoy fevah. She done fergit us all, suh." Phebe covered her face with her apron and cried softly.

Cooper leaned, sick and silent, against the house. He remembered in a flash that she had been bareheaded as she ran by him the night before—that she had no wrap about her light evening gown, no protection against the treacherous damp of spring. And he had let her go, in his childish fit of spleen and wounded self-love !

His voice was thin and hollow as he turned again to the old servant.

"Can I do anything; any little thing, even, to help, Phebe?" he said.

"Oh, no, suh; thank you kindly, suh. Evyting ben looked foh. Mis' Weston ben hyar, an' Mis' Denison. Dey done look out foh evyting. She done speak yo' name dis maw'n, suh. She done speak it twice, but now she fergit us all, an' talk, talk, talk 'bout de Kernal, like he was hyar still. Oh, befoh de Lord, ef de Kernal was hyar fer jess a little, *he* done make her well."

Cooper left the porch and went unsteadily to the gate. Oh, the ghastly beauty and freshness of everything! The river sparkled, and how green the fields lay, stretching against the base of the south hill! He saw things, as he hurried aimlessly along, but all under a film of nightmare. She would die and it would be he who killed her,—he with his silly, wicked, childish pride. And she had called his name that very

morning, when he perhaps was sleeping
—dreaming of assured success. And it
was small wonder she spoke of him no
more, but called for the dead. Better
call for the dead Colonel. He had
never let her risk her life, to gratify a
senseless pride. He had been a man, a
a man, a man !

It was well that Cooper's course lay
away from the village among the meadows, whither he had unwittingly turned,
for he was little better than a madman,
muttering, crying out, tossing his hands
as he went.

After a long half hour, calmer but
wild looking and haggard, he came to
the river-bank, to the spot where stood
the oak upon which he had once cut the
initials of the woman he loved.

Half asleep in the slanting sunlight,
his back propped against an outcrop-
ping root from the great tree that
shaded the deep water of " Denison's
Hole," lay a man. It was Ezra Spicer,
the village outcast and drunkard, popu-

lar with parents as a warning, and furtively beloved by many a boy for his
kind offices in the gentle art of angling.

As Cooper stopped and stood a moment near him, Ezra turned, nodded in
a friendly way, and resumed watching
his float. Presently he turned again
and looked more carefully at the other.

"Ye aint sick, be ye, Dick?" he asked
gently.

"No, Ezra," replied Cooper, with a
forced laugh; "only played out—tired
out—no sleep lately."

Ezra shook his head. "Wal, I s'pose
that's from too much lawin'. I used
to worry some myself till I took to
fishin'. Set down, wont ye?"

Cooper shook his head. "Wal, 't is
damp, bad weather fer chills an' ager.
Say—there's sickness up to Mis' Callander's. Is it Mis' Callander herself?
'T is, hey! Wal, now, as I was goin'
home last night, I seen some one settin' by the bridge-end nighest Kernal

Callander's, no shawl ner bonnet on, cryin'—oh, cryin' so I could hear her; —an' I kind o' thought she looked like Mis' Callander, an' I told Liza so. She said I wa'n't in no fit way to see who 't was, an' mebbe that 's so ; but I sez to myself, whoever 't was, ' it 's a bad time fer chills and ager,' an' I—" Suddenly across the speaker's slow-moving mind came the recollection of the reports that were in many quarters, of Cooper's devotion to Madam Callander. He broke off his rambling talk at once, drew his line in with great comparative activity, and examined the bait. "I thought I had a bite just now, an' I guess I *did*," he said, then turning, saw that Cooper was walking swiftly along the river-path towards the bridge. "Wal, I *am* a derned bass-wood fool," he muttered to himself. "So 't was Mis' Callander—an' she was lookin' fer some one too—an' I guess Dick Cooper aint fur from his name, nuther."

So certain facts from circumstantial evidence passed into local history.

V.

Mrs. Callander did not die, but recovery was very slow. As time went on, indeed, it was whispered that recovery would never be complete. Cooper was as regular each day at the Callander house, as the doctor himself. From Phebe he was able to learn the daily news with moderate exactness. She had long known his secret and suspected her mistress's inclinations. She scorned her husband's forebodings as to change of name without change of initial letter, partly because she disagreed with any statement dogmatically advanced by Marcus. Again and again Cooper would ask her, " Does she ever speak my name, or mention me ? " And at first Phebe answered truthfully, but as the weeks ran on and convalescence began slowly to assert itself, and no name of man but that of Ewen Callander passed the sick woman's lips, the negress in sheer pity drew upon her fancy.

"Oh, yas, honey, she done speak ob *yo'*—foh suah; yas suh, yas, indeed," and poor Cooper would go home comforted.

At last the doctor announced that Madam Callander might again see her friends, and Cooper, meeting Dr. Graham, asked leave to call. The doctor looked at him in such a way that the other saw he understood his anxiety and its cause and then said, "She should have nothing to excite her."

"Well—perhaps—well, I can wait, I can wait," said Dick. The tone of disappointment in his voice touched the doctor's heart. He was an elderly man, a cousin of Cooper's father, and Dick's love affair was well known to him.

"No," he said hesitatingly, a curious look upon his face, "I think you may go, in fact you 'd better go as soon as you can."

Cooper thanked him and went his way wondering somewhat at the doctor's words, but that same afternoon found him at the gate of the Callander house, his heart beating almost to pain, his hands cold and nerveless. He saw Phebe upon the porch. She showed him into the drawing-room, answering his questions in a way that seemed to him constrained and unnatural.

Everything in the great, dim room spoke to him of his past, his past so brief a time gone by, but so remote. He had no set speech this day to utter. He had parted with what little artificiality he had once assumed. . . .

She was coming—he heard the rustle of skirts, the tap, tap, of feet upon the stair, a shadow crossed the threshold of the door, and now she herself stood there. He sprang forward, both his hands outstretched, a voiceless cry in his throat ;—then he dropped his hands to his side.

She was not greatly changed physically, thinner of course, and the roses not yet in her cheeks. Her beautiful hair, which had not been sacrificed, was drawn as of old from her low white forehead, her eyes were bright and blue as ever, and she was smiling.

But in those eyes, not one ray beyond the light of mere recognition shone; in that smile sedate and kindly, were only complaisance and the half condescension she had displayed to the Richard Cooper of years before. As he stood in frozen silence she came toward him.

" It's Mr. Cooper, is it not," she said, as she put out her hand, " and when did *you* return?" He murmured some response and sank into a chair she pointed to.

"It is your vacation, I suppose," she went on, in a voice as passionless and devoid of remembrance as falling water. Then in the same weird echo of words she had spoken once before she said.

" You will find many changes."

" I find them," he said hoarsely. She stared a moment, rather at his voice than at the words, then rising, went towards the mantle-shelf.

"That is an excellent portrait of him," she said. "Ah, what a man he was and what a loss to Dorset." . . .

Cooper never could recall without a shudder the few minutes that elapsed before he could make his farewells. Stunned and heartbroken he found his way to the village. In the broad shady street near the church he again met Doctor Graham. "Dick," called the latter. Cooper went to him.

"Did she know you?" said the doctor bluntly.

Cooper looked at him, flushed, and turned away. "Yes," he answered stiffly.

"Stop," called the other. "Dick, this *is* my business even if *you* don't think so. Your secret's no secret to me, and I must ask you what I do, as a doctor. Now, tell me; how much had she forgotten?"

"Forgotten!" cried Cooper bitterly,

"oh, Doctor, Doctor, she 'd forgotten all I hoped she might remember."

He took hold of the muddy spokes of the wheel and swayed himself backwards and forwards in his anguish, the tears streaming down his face. The old man put a kind hand upon his shoulder. "Dick," he said, "be a man. She never *will* remember, I 'm afraid, my boy—but be a man, make new memories, don't give up." Cooper shook his head and turned away. He knew that a little divine spark that glows but once for every man and woman, had gone out. He felt that some memories once lost are never replaced, and he was but too right.

VI.

Madam Callander never caught up the lost stitches. What power of loving had been in her in that time so vanished, so effaced, seemed now changed to a morbid devotion to her dead husband, a devotion that excluded all things else. It must not be thought that Cooper at once abandoned hope. But during the several occasions following, upon which he saw Madam Callander, she was so oblivious of him in any character but that of young Dick Cooper, the lawyer, that he eventually gave way. Other aspirants for her hand in the course of the next few years appeared, but he felt no envy. He knew what the result must be. And their rejections were so final in character, so abrupt in manner, that suitors grew wary. Whereas Madam Callander had once been wont to say "no" courteously, sometimes compassionately, her present attitude was one of indignation upon being asked to take a successor to the Colonel. It was incomprehensible to her, either that she should be considered by any chance in the way to be comforted, or that any man should deem himself worthy to fill Colonel Callander's place. As time went on, her old predilection for Cooper

had a sort of shadowy revival in a de-
cided liking she grew to have for him.
She was glad to have him call upon her
—she used to confide in him.

He had become a rather prematurely-
old looking man with serious eyes, and
an expression half quizzical, half sad.
He would listen to her by the hour
while she talked of the Colonel's merits
and of the past. It cut him to the
heart at first, but he grew used to it.
And it was a joy in a half tragic way,
merely to sit and watch her, and to
know that she was really his, his own,
if but those chords of memory should
once awaken.

So years drifted by. With the Mexican war a regiment was formed in the
Southern Tier, and Cooper went out as
captain of a company. He distin-
guished himself at Molino del Rey and
again at Chapultepec, and two years
later returned, a major, to Dorset. He
had contemplated exchanging into the
regular service, certain influences being

powerful at his back, but the tendrils of the past were too strong to break, and the desire to be near his love too keen to resist. Had he been formally rejected, had he found that he had never been loved, he could not have remained in his native town. But—he *had* been loved ; she was *his*, though she could not know it, could not be told of it, and he would stay as near her side as he was permitted and never leave her again.

He never did.

Years went and came. Cooper grew gray and somewhat infirm. Time treated him with no more than ordinary deference, but it touched Madame Callander lightly and lovingly. She never entirely lost her beauty.

She grew more prone, as she grew older, to prattle of the Colonel. She treated Cooper upon his return from Mexico, bringing honor and title, with great respect, and the gray-haired Major with his patient sad eyes would listen to her, twice a week, with military regularity, as she spoke of the well-known past, *her* past and the Colonel's. He never failed to assent to any eulogy of the departed, however extravagant, and Madam Callander once said that he was the only man in Dorset who had not been jealous of her husband.

The garden of her memory was grown up to old-time flowers, like a country door-yard, where pinks, and hollyhocks, and dahlias, and peonies bloom and thrive.

VII.

She died suddenly, almost painlessly. Her maid Phebe, a woman past eighty years of age, was by her side. The negress heard her mistress say softly to herself part of the church service, and saw her suddenly raise herself in the bed and put her hands to her eyes. The old woman leaned over towards her and as she did her mistress flung herself with a sob upon her breast.

" Oh, Phebe, Phebe, he has gone," she

cried. " I 've lost him, I 've lost him."
The memory so long asleep had
wakened.

The two women, the black and the
white, whose hair time had turned the
same shade, and whose hearts had been
always of a color, sobbed together in
the darkness of the sick-room.

Presently Madam Callander slipped
back upon her pillow. She was quiet a
moment, murmured something to herself, quivered, and then lay still. . . .

This Phebe told to Major Cooper,
and during the rest of the day, and the
next, to the hour of the obsequies, his
face wore a look serene and happy, such
a look as had not been upon it for many
years. Some people wondered at this,
and said that age turns blood cold, and
when the Major, though he went to the
church, refused to go to the grave, un-
kind things were said. But they did
not touch him in any way. He had
pondered upon the matter, and he could
not get himself to see the woman he

had loved so truly and for so long laid by the dust of a man he felt had not the real right. He had loved her longer than Ewen Callander. He had loved her a lifetime, and now she must sleep by the side of a man whose un-awakened wife she had been.

He did not follow to the grave, but went instead to the river-bank, to the old oak he knew and loved. From his pocket he took a chisel and hammer and recut the letters, almost untrace-able now from the outgrowth of bark. Then, below, he put his own initials. He had the right now at the last, for at the last she had returned to him.

The Expiation of Ezra Spicer.

III

The Expiation of Ezra Spicer.

I.

THE sun of early June was two hours above the highest pines along the ridge of the south hill. The slanting rays lighted the shallow waters of the Connedaga and lured the fish from pools below the banks into the riffles. The steers and yearlings in the Denison meadows, straying in various directions from their night huddle, were laying with steadfast industry foundations for their noon-tide cuds. The milkers were reappearing from the lane which led to the great gambrel-roofed red barn, and with their lowing mingled at times the distant bay of a hound.

The valley of the Connedaga was at
its best—the day was growing in
beauty—but there was one at least
from whom the smile of nature gained
no response. Among the hazel shoots
that set up their screen along the river
course, and filled like a tapestried web
the spaces between the trees, crouched
a negro—a man of middle age, whose
intelligent, almost gentle, face was piti-
fully wrought upon by terror. He was
gasping hoarsely for breath and his
eyes were fixed with painful eagerness
upon the skirt of wood about the base
of MacRae's Hill. Presently, his wind
partly restored, but still panting deeply,
he slipped into the stream, pushed rapidly across, the water about his knees,
and disappeared among the alders on
the other bank. A minute later he
reappeared in the meadow a few rods
beyond, and ran, stooping, along its
border, keeping in the half shelter of a
fence of stumps. At a point in the
stream perhaps a quarter of a mile from

where he first entered it he once more
took to the river. As he waded
towards the middle of the current the
water came about his hips ; when he
neared the other bank only his head
was visible, and this was soon lost to
view, beneath an overhanging bush
whose branches dipped to the river's
brim.

At this moment a group of four men,
one of them mounted, another a negro
with a dog in leash, came at a brisk
trot from the woods below MacRae's
Hill and in a few moments, led by the
dog who strained eagerly at his leash
and ran with nose to earth, they
reached the spot where the fugitive
had first taken to the stream. Here
they paused. For a few moments they
talked earnestly while the dog, a kindly-
faced type of the beagle family, having
ranged a yard or two up and down the
bank, stood at fault, nose in air, belling
musically into the wind. Then the
mounted man spurred his horse into

the water, ordered the others to follow and the company were presently upon the opposite shore, when a clamor from the hound showed the trail once more established.

A short digression is needed to explain the presence of a scene like the one described—within the boundaries of New York State. . . .

II.

When Major Norris, late of Dinwiddie County, Virginia, attracted by the ardent representations of his friend Colonel Callander, followed the great waterway of the Susquehanna to remote Pulteney County, he brought with him a large household of blacks.

A score of years went pleasantly by in the pursuit of such pleasures as the little backwoods county-seat afforded before the Major found need and leisure to count the cost. When at last he did so, he discovered himself face to face

with facts as unpleasant as creditors—
and harder to shun. He had run his
horses into premature old age, and himself into inextricable debt. His farm
—plantation he chose to call it—was
heavily mortgaged, and his only unin-
cumbered property a score of " likely "
negroes. Such of these as were needful
to the Major as grooms or house servants lived upon his place, and were de-
pendents upon his kitchen—but nearly
half of them had long been in practical
emancipation. Major Norris, in his days
of prosperity, was an easy master and
permitted such of his " people " as he
had no immediate employment for to
toil for themselves, live in their own
way, and enjoy the fruits of their labor.

But with the coming of the evil day,
and the final departure of the last hours
of credit, the Major turned his eyes, although regretfully, upon his servants—
whose market-value, in Maryland or Virginia, might yet recoup him, and bridge
the way to better days. What hesita-

tion he felt at the outset vanished promptly when the rumors came with continually increasing volume that the State of New York was about to free all negroes within its limits.

As yet it had done little more than forbid the traffic in slaves and provide for the gradual emancipation of children of slave parents born within the State after Independence Day, 1799. The exportation of slaves was also forbidden, though a master removing permanently from the State, by observing certain legal formalities, might take his slaves with him.

It was still remembered—twenty-five years ago—by the oldest inhabitant, how, one by one, the negroes of the Norris's household disappeared, ostensibly to be employed upon a farm said to be owned by the Major near the Pennsylvania line. And long time in the ears of the early inhabitants echoed the indignation that arose from a whisper to a full-voiced outcry, when the Major, relying upon his prerogative of master, began to impress for the same farm service the negroes who had been permitted by him to enjoy for years a half-freedom.

This indignation however was mainly among the younger men—Cyrus Weston, Richard Cooper and others of their age—or rough-and-ready rustic characters like Captain Ball, whose upland farm to the south of the roll-way hill had served more than once as a refuge for fugitive blacks. The older, more conservative and perhaps more representative men in Dorset belonged to two sorts. Men like Judge Barton, who took an Old Testament view of slavery, while guarding a conscience and morality of the strictest New England type, and others who with Colonel Calander opposed anything approaching radicalism and a further extension of the rights of man—even then encroaching, as the honest Colonel held, upon the rights of men. As yet too—though no

one doubted its speedy enactment—
emancipation was still in the future.
The opposition, therefore, which Major
Norris had to combat was hardly more
than passive and he urged his enterprise with the energy of a man whose
time is limited and whose conscience is
clear—for it is only fair to say that the
Major, fully believing that he possessed
all the rights of a Virginia master, had no
doubts as to the probity of his conduct,
though he regretted its necessity.

Two days previous to the morning
upon which this chronicle opens, a
burly, keen-eyed, fat-faced man, well-
dressed, but with the look of a drover
in broadcloth, took lodging at the Eagle
Tavern, signing himself Captain Faxon,
Culpepper, Virginia. He was no stranger to John Silsbee, the proprietor.
Twice before had the Captain visited
Dorset, and on each occasion addi-
tional harvesters had been needed at
Major Norris's somewhat mythical farm
upon the Pennsylvania border.

On the following day it was known
that Carter Sampson, a negro nominally
the property of Major Norris, but for
years practically a free man, had left
his home and was supposed to be in
hiding.

Now Carter Sampson was already possessed of a small competence—he was
a leading member of the negro contin-
gent in the congregation over which
Parson Knowles was established, and
he had many friends among the poor,
both white and black, by reason of his
unpretending charity.

It is a curious commentary upon the
time, however, that no measures were
taken to block Faxon's activities. The
slave-trader, for so he actually was, possessed a certain diplomacy and cunning
that carried him unimpeded along the
line of his efforts. To his mind Sampson was as much an animal and a chat-
tel as the beagle the trader had borrowed
to track him, but he half met the gen-
eral disapproval of his quest by dwell-

ing, with men of the better element in Dorset, upon the injustice of a man's not being allowed to do as he would with his own,—and among the less respectable by a profuse hospitality dispensed before the " Eagle " bar. He had obtained some assistance on his other visits by the liberal use of money, and it was by bribing that he had induced the negro, Lucas John, a man of great strength and personal courage though of little principle, to assist him ; a treachery to his color that was for years bitterly laid up against the black. It was through this renegade's information, and by his assistance, that Faxon, with two white followers, stablemen in the Major's employ, laid the beagle's nose to a true scent this morning in June, 18—.

III.

Ezra Spicer had half filled his pail with suckers, and was beginning to meditate upon a homeward course. It was four o'clock in the afternoon, and by the time he could reach the Eagle tavern, whither, in funds or not, he invariably repaired at the day's close, it would be nearly supper-time. He had seen Faxon and his following that morning beating the undergrowth of the swampy meadows a quarter of a mile from his fishing-ground, and then had lost them, as the cry of the hound sounded fainter in the distance. In the early afternoon he had sought another fishing-hole, almost opposite the spot where Sampson for a second time had entered the stream. And here he sat, with his eyes intent upon his float, when the trample of feet in the cleared field behind him caused him to look quickly around.

The Virginian and his companions were returning empty-handed from the chase. The tired hound no longer tugged at the leash, and Faxon wearied and thirsty from his long quest, was in an evil temper. He cursed frequently, and with no apparent reason, and rode sullenly in front of his party. As he caught sight of the fisherman he pulled in his horse and stared at him. The renegade negro Lucas, discovering Spicer at the same time, ran to Faxon's side and said a few words hurriedly in an undertone; then he came to the worm fence that separated the field from the river bank and accosted Ezra.

"Aint seed no one passin', has you, Ezry?" he asked with a shamefaced grin.

"Seen you an' yer crowd this mornin'," said Spicer, shortly.

"Ye aint happened to see any o' Major Norris's folks?"

Ezra shook his head.

"Wal, now, dat 's extr'odny," said Lucas, with a glance towards Faxon. "We foun' tracks like dey was Carter Sampson's dis maw'n' jist across from dis yer place, an' den we lose 'em— done look all day down de rivah an' we caint someways pick em' up."

Faxon, who had got from his horse, came to the side of the negro.

"Cap'n Faxon, dis yer's Mist' Spisah, he knows de rivah, knows it well, suh."

"Reckon you'd like to make a little money, an' make it right easy, my man?" said Faxon. Ezra gazed straight before him and did not reply. He had already, the night before, been approached by one of Norris's men, and, while he had refused to be of active aid, the thought of the easy money had teased his memory the entire day. "All you've got to do," said Faxon persuasively, "is to give us a quiet tip. If he came this way,—you saw him. Now just tell me where and when. I'll take care of the rest, and you get well paid ; is it a bargain ?"

While he was speaking there was a sudden sound beneath the bank as of an animal moving softly in the still water of the hole. Ezra's eyes turned swiftly upon the screen of bushes that reached out its green arms above the water. His first thought was that the noise had been made by one of the colony of water-rats that inhabited the locality, but an instant's glance was enough to show him a man—a negro, Carter Sampson—the water almost covering his head, his chilled lips quivering piteously and his eyes gleaming through the covert of leaves, fixed upon Spicer with a mute, despairing appeal.

"Well," said Faxon, "what do you say!"

"I aint seen him Cap'n," said Ezra huskily; "I aint seen no one."

"Come, come," said the other. "Of course you have, and you 're helping cheat a gentleman of his property by not lending a hand now—and talk of seeing things, look at this!" Ezra's eyes, do what he could, turned upon the tempter. A bright piece of gold representing more than Spicer ever at any one time had possessed, shone in Faxon's palm. "Look at that; think what that would git ye. There 's a power of good times and good whiskey in that—think of it."

Ezra *had* thought of such a thing before ; all the long morning he had striven to convince himself that his refusal of the day before, to assist in the capture of the fugitive Sampson, was better than renewed credit and a hearty welcome at the tavern. "So help me God !" he said again, but still with his eyes upon the coin, "I aint seen no one at all."

The Captain withdrew his hand slowly, and suddenly the unhappy Spicer struck a hasty bargain with the devil. He could not, in cold blood point out the hidden negro trembling almost within touch of him ; and he could not face the disappearance of that shining fortune. "I haint seen him," he reiterated, " but," in a lower voice and with half a nod towards the water below him, "you better look under the banks where the deep holes be, that's my advice." A sickening

sense made up of disappointment and
remorse came over him as the coin was
slipped back into the Captain's breeches.
" Good advice," said Faxon shortly ;
" no market here for advice though ;
reckon *I* know enough to hunt him out
if he 's around." He turned with an im-
patient curse, and with Lucas rejoined
his party.

It was the good fortune of the man
in the water that Faxon had not seen
the half nod which Spicer directed
toward the pool, and that annoyance
at what seemed the fisherman's ob-
stinacy took the Captain in a pet from
the spot. That nod, however, had not
escaped the fugitive's eye. In a few
moments the dog broke out into a yelp,
and the group turned with renewed
interest into a patch of timber, and disappeared. The good angel had his
wing about Sampson, and the demon of
remorse sat side by side with Ezra
Spicer as he again flung his line into
the stream. " Let 'em go," he said

aloud, "they 'll git nothin' from me."
He gazed shamefacedly at the screen of
bushes above the eddying water, then
looked quickly away. The eyes were
still there; the glance was that of a
frightened animal, but it was full, as
well, of scorn unutterable. Spicer
turned hot from head to foot. That
glance was as loud as a cry.

The yelp of the hound in the distance had changed to a steady bay.
Ezra despite his shame could not resist
a chuckle. "They've struck Stanbro's
Run, I guess," he said again aloud. "I
seen fox tracks there this mornin'. If
they will use fox-dogs they must expec'
to have 'em chase foxes." The pursuit
same suddenly into view, several meadows distant, the hound, escaped from
his leash, running free, and Faxon following alone at a canter. "They tell
me them Virginny folks is great on fox
huntin'," chuckled Ezra. "Wal, he 's
after one now, I guess, an' there 'll be
no more man huntin' fer a spell."

He looked shyly towards the hidden
man as he said this, and laughed in a
tentative, deprecating way. The silence
of deep contempt brooded above the
pool and Spicer's soul writhed within
him. He was *sure* now that Sampson
had seen his attempted treason. For a
few minutes longer he strove to fish,
but the thought of those scornful eyes,
that he felt still burned upon him from
the bush curtain below, seared his conscience as with a white-hot iron. At
last he rose, gathered up his pail and
bait-can, and climbed the fence into the
cleared lot. Then, as though checked by
a sudden thought, he turned, came back
again to the bank, reseated himself and
began again to fish. This time he devoted himself to his occupation, keeping
his eyes resolutely before him. For
awhile he sat as though utterly unmind-
ful of another's presence. Suddenly he
looked round as though a sound had
caught his ear, then jumping up he ran
to the fence. "What!" he called, as

though in reply to a hail. "No! no! I aint seen him yit. No—he haint showed himself 'long here, sence ye left. What! Oh, all right! Tell the Captain I've got my eye on that coin yit —all right!"

A crow on the limb of a buttonwood took cognizance of this sudden clamor and winged lazily towards the hill; a woodchuck, seated as nearly midway between the two doors to his burrow as he was able to estimate, ran to one entrance and sat up, looking enquiringly towards the bank. The cattle in the adjacent meadows heard but paid no notice to the shouts. No other living creature was visible and Faxon and his henchmen were some two miles away upon the trail of a widely peripatetic dog-fox.

Ezra returned to his seat beside the river and resumed fishing. One deprived of the use of his eyes would have gathered that chance had brought the pursuers back within earshot of the fisherman—that they had again sought information, and had been sent upon their way in ignorance.

That the only human being within reach of Ezra's monologue thought so was presently apparent. A brief time had elapsed since Spicer last resumed his rod, when a splash sounded beneath the bank and the head and shoulders of Sampson appeared through the bushes. "Ezry," he whispered, "are dey gone?" His eyes had lost their hostile glitter and were once more friendly and trustful. Spicer saw the change and his heart leaped. He had only for a moment yielded to the tempter, and his feeble but kindly nature had already suffered keenly from remorse. "All clear, Carter—all clear," he said briskly, taking the black's hand and helping him up the bank. "Climb up here and lie out in the sun. Gosh, how wet ye be—got a good right to be, I guess—been in *all day!* Crotch all hemlock! Jest get them clothes off, and I 'll wring em out."

When Sampson had struggled out of his wet garments the repentant Spicer wrung them as best he could and hung them where the slanting sun could reach them. Then he came to the negro who was stretched shivering upon the grass. "Be ye hungry?" said he; "here's a little lunch I got left." Sampson with eager thanks seized it and ate ravenously. "I aint eat since las' night," he said finally. "An' I 'se feah'd I 'se gwine to have chills an' agah." Then he opened one hand which he had held closed, and displayed a five-dollar piece. "Ezry," he said, "will ye go to town for me, an' git me a blanket an' a shirt—an' a little whiskey too?" Ezra got briskly to his feet. "Course I will, Carter," he said, "ef ye kin trust me with all that cash."

He blushed suddenly, for it was a coin of the same denomination as that which Faxon had shown him half an hour before. Then, as the negro hastened to assure him of his confidence and put

133

the money into his hand, he said, looking steadfastly towards the hill and
avoiding the other's eyes. "Ye did n't
think I was goin' to tell on ye to Faxon
just now did ye, Carter?" Sampson
hesitated a moment. "Yas, Ezry," he
said presently, " fer a while I did ; yas, I
did, but praise de Lord, I was mistook
—yas, praise de Lord ! When I heah'd
you call to de Cap'n de secon' time,
den I knew I was wrong." Ezra had
climbed the worm-fence and was about
to start homewards. " Carter," he said,
still looking anywhere but in the
negro's face, " don't you never fear fer
Ezry Spicer ; they 'll git nuthin' from
me," he went on, and this time he felt
that the truth was in his heart, "an'
I 'll be back soon 's dark. Better run up
and down back of them saplings an' git
warm. Ol' Faxon wont be back this
way soon. I know that there fox he 's
a chasin', an' it lives in the nex'
county ! "

IV.

It was characteristic of Ezra Spicer that he should make the whiskey the first of his purchases. Aside from the ordinary magnetism the threshold of the Eagle Tavern exerted upon his feet he had a natural desire to display himself before Silsbee as a purchaser, with ready cash. He turned lovingly in his pocket the coin which Sampson had given him, and pictured old John Silsbee's surprise when he heard it ring upon the bar. One thing he had determined upon, and that was that none of the material benefits of wealth should come to himself through this money. He felt that a divine interposition had saved him from the basest treachery, and that he owed utter and complete reparation to Carter Sampson —reparation, which from its completeness should, in a way, approach expiation.

He entered the Eagle Tavern with

an important air, in spite of his humbled condition of mind, and accosted Silsbee as the latter stood behind the bar, his back towards the door.

"I'd like a quart of whiskey, Mr. Silsbee," he said with an attempt at nonchalance.

"Guess ye would," said Silsbee dryly, not lifting his eyes from a book in whose pages were marshalled an array of ill-formed figures representing such aridity in Dorset as received credit. "Guess ye most always would, Ezry." Spicer spun the coin nosily upon the bar; the tavern-keeper looked quickly up. His eyes went from Ezra's face to the gold piece and back again several times and finally fixed themselves with an angry glance upon the man. "Wal," said Spicer, a trifle disquieted by the other's manner, "are ye goin' to let me have that whiskey?"

"Where did ye git that money?"

"Wal, that's my bizniss, I guess!"

"Where did ye git it, I say? See

here, Ezry Spicer, you hain't been takin'
that there Faxon's money to hunt
down Sampson have ye? Ef ye have,
by the Lord Harry, I 'll never—— "

" Wal, now Silsbee," said Spicer back-
ing away from the bar, "of course I
haint; why, how you talk! Sampson 's
been a good friend to me allus; of course
I haint teched the Cap'n's money, so
help me John Rogers! You kin ask
him when he comes in to-night. Why,
you aint got no call to holler; you 're a
boardin' him! "

" That 's different," said Silsbee quickly. " Boardin' folks is my bizniss, an'
nigger huntin' aint your'n. Wal, I 'll
take yer word fer it; pooty coin! " He
spun it into the air and caught it as he
spoke, then flung it into a cash drawer;
"I wisht I could see a few more of
'em."

Ezra watched the decanting of the
whiskey from a keg behind the counter,
and in his parched condition envied the
functions of the funnel. "Wisht' my

throat was that there tin thing," he
muttered to himself; then sighing
deeply he crossed the room and looked
steadily out of the rear window. He
knew that Silsbee would offer him a
horn of the whiskey, after filling the
bottle, as he usually did in the case of
patrons who purchased in quantity, and
he could not face refusing it. To his
quaint sense of right and justice it had
seemed to him from the first that to
touch a drop of his favorite beverage,
brought to his reach by means of the
money of a man whom, for a brief moment, he had thought to betray, would
be almost unbearable. It was now an
impossibility, since the scathing manner
of the inn-keeper—all the more scathing
because adopted by a man for whom
Ezra himself had no great respect.
And yet he felt, should he return to
the side of the bar, see the little tumbler turn amber as the Monongahela
brimmed it, and smell the fragrance
of the rye, that even the impossible

might be surmounted. So he remained
by the window watching abstractedly
the life in a paddock at the rear of the
tavern. " Ezry," said Silsbee presently,
" here 's a drop of the stuff, just a sample
to show ye it 's all right."

" No, I—no, thank ye—not now—no
—well—say, Silsbee," said Spicer, des-
perately evading the temptation, " that
duckwing game of your 'n has lost a
spur, haint he?" "What?" said Silsbee,
who was a keen sportsman and looked
upon cock-fighting as justifiable under
certain circumstances; if two birds happened to meet in Squire Weston's cow-
shed, for example. " Let 's see 'im."
He started to leave the bar by a little
door at one end—" Say, jest fetch my
bottle along, will ye," said Ezra, and in
a moment it was in his keeping.
" Where 's that duckwing?" said Silsbee. " Oh, why he got both spurs all
right—ye must be gittin' blind, Ezra;
here 's yer change." Spicer took the
money and started for the door.

"What's yer hurry? Ye haint had yer drink yet." Ezra made no reply, and in a moment the puzzled tavern-keeper saw him go rapidly past the porch towards the stores.

V.

It was not far from nine o'clock when Ezra Spicer, a bundle in his arms and a quart bottle of whiskey bulging one of his jacket-pockets, took his way through the Cooper meadows to the river. The moon was not yet atop the hill though its light already was outlining against the sky the pines that fringed the summit. He walked rapidly but stealthily. He did not wish to be seen, for he was a personage upon the river-bank to whom any lad in Dorset would eagerly join himself in hope of learning from a master the gentle art of night-lines. He had already, in the early evening, refused to explain to certain of the youth of Dorset his theory of eel-traps, for his present mission demanded secrecy.

As he came to the river a flare of light shone round a bend above him, and half a dozen boys with pronged spears and torches came into view. Convinced that the negro would see the peril which the blazing pine knots would in-evitably bring upon him and retire into the meadow, but resolved, none the less, to take no chances, Ezra dropped his bundle and ran out upon a spit of shingle that stretched towards the mid-dle of the river. "Hello, Ezry!" came a chorus—"say, we're havin' great luck—(there he goes, Dan, quick! Gosh, he's a big one!) Say, Ezry, show us where ye got the big shiner last week, will ye?" "No, I wont," said Spicer promptly, "unless ye come out o' that still water; ye'll be in my eel-lines in a minute. Come ashore an' I'll tell ye where the big shiners be." The lads came splashing and scram-bling to the bank. "Now, then," said

Ezra, with the air of a man on his own property, "jest ye cut across the medder there, to the bend where the riffles be. Under the alders, where the water's deep an' swift, too, ye'll git the big shiners. Now run along—I aint goin' to let ye see where my night-lines be—run along!"

The boys were midway of the meadow, heading eagerly towards the alders, when Ezra wading hip-deep across the quiet water reached the bank a few rods above the spot of Sampson's conceal-ment. Then he went softly along the meadow path and called. In a moment Sampson came forward. "Thank de Lord," he said fervently, "thank de Lord, you've come back, Ezry!" There was something in his tone that to Spicer's conscience indicated that a fear had lingered in Sampson's mind of the entire fidelity of his white friend, and the fisherman's face burned in the darkness. He *had* been *proud* of his abstinence at the tavern—he was now *glad* as well. " Wal, Carter," he said busily, " it 's 'bout time to git a movin'. Here 's the blanket an' the flannel shirt. Why, yer breeches is most dry! An' here 's some crackers an' cheese I stole from Liza. Put 'em in yer pockets an' eat 'em as ye travel. An' here 's the whiskey. Now ye aint got much time, fer the moon 's comin' over ol' Baldy. Why, man, yer shiverin' yit. Take a good drink o' this." The negro took a few swallows of the liquor—then put the bottle down. " Dey 's a pain in my chest," he said coughing, " an' de roomatiz in my hip am pow'ful bad to-night. I 'se gwine rub me wiv de whiskey stid o' drinkin' it." " What!" said Ezra, almost sternly—" rub yerself with Monongahela?"—" Deed I is, Ezry," said Sampson simply. " I donc do dat befor', plenty times."

" Wal, by gosh," said Spicer leaning against the fence, watching the external application of the liquor with ill-concealed disapproval, " ef ye 'd said what ye wanted it fer I 'd a' got rotgut. Why, Carter, that there 's Mononga-hela! D' ye understand?"

The negro was too busy to reply—pouring the spirits freely into his broad hands, chafing his hip vigorously and treating his chest in a like manner. At last he put the bottle down with a sigh of evident relief, and drew on his new flannel shirt. "Now, Ezry," he said presently, "if ye 'll direct me to Cap'n Ball's, I 'll be goin' along, an' God be praise', an' thank ye!" Ezra gave the required information, while making up the fugitive's bundle. "It 's a tough climb," said he, "an' it 's steep —but you 'll git to the wood-road all right, an' then all 's plain sailin'. Don't ye be afeard o' the wolves—they aint hungry, nor they aint plenty this spring, an' take care ye don't slide down the roll-way hill."

He slipped the bottle into the bundle as he ended speaking. Sampson stooped over, took it out, saw there were but a couple of inches left, and put it by Spicer's side. "It 'll be broke in de climb," he said; "I don' counten'ce de use of ahjus licohs gen'lly, but you dun get wet crossin' de river; you kin take it, Ezry." "I don't want it," said Spicer, roughly and with a sort of desperation. It seemed to him that temptation, this day, was relentless as fate. "An' here 's a dollar change fer ye that I forgot," he said, suddenly remembering its existence. Sampson reached out to take it, then withdrew his hand. "Ezry," he said, "dat 's foh you. Don' yo' refuse me, for it 's balm to mah conscience. For, Ezry, I dun mak' a mistake an' errah 'bout yo' dis mawn'. I dun mak' a misjustice. An' when I heah'd yo' settin' de boys away from de rivah an' seed yo' tak' all this trouble foh me—I—yes—it 's balm for mah conscience, deed it is." He gripped Ezra's hand suddenly with real feeling, climbed the fence, and was soon out of sight in the darkness.

Ezra sat still for some minutes on the grass by the side of the river. He realized with renewed shame that he had not been strong enough vigorously to refuse the gifts pressed upon him, but he told himself again and again that he would not, come what might, profit by them. After a while he rose, looked at the whiskey bottle, which seemed to jeer at him from the side of the fence, then, with an impulse he could not restrain, he picked it up, clambered into the pasture lot and took a homeward course. He was tired and chilled —and there, in his very hand, was panacea for weariness and cold. He had already resisted the tempter, and the tempter had not fled. After all, where was the harm? One drink—that's all that was left—and he had not, really— anyhow, only for a second—meant harm to Sampson. Why, the negro would n't grudge the drop of liquor even if he knew all!

With a quick movement he lifted the

flask to his lips, and at the same moment his foot slid into the burrow of a
woodchuck and he fell prostrate. When
he picked himself up the bottle was
still in his hands and the remnant of
whiskey unspilled. He gave it but a
glance, then poured it deliberately into
the hole that had thrown him. " It
wan't meant I should have it," he said,
with a superstitious shake of his head.
"*You* kin have it, ye basswood ground-
hog. I hope ye'll take to it,—that's
the wust I kin wish ye—an' here's the
bottle fer yer family to smell!" He
dropped the empty flask, as a supple-
ment to this irony, into the burrow of
the slumbering rodent, and again resumed his way, crossing the river at the
shallows, a quarter of a mile distant.
As he neared the Eagle Tavern he was
conscious once more of a stress of spirit.
The Mexican dollar given him by
Sampson burned in his pocket. As it
touched his fingers he seemed to feel
the devil jog his elbow. But he was

stronger now than before his last temptation. He passed the tavern door
with head averted, quickened his pace
into a trot, and in a few moments
reached his own abode. There he took
the coin from his pocket, and, without
looking at it, carried it to a corner of
the shabby room and hid it beneath a
chest. " Thank God ! " he said suddenly ; " to-morrer 's the Sabbath," a
sentiment new to the lips of Ezra
Spicer, and prompted rather by the reason that the tavern would be closed,
than that the house of worship would
be open. Then he went to bed, but
not to slumber.

It was almost morning when Ezra,
who had not yet closed his eyes in
sleep, arose and went to the chest
under which the coin was hidden. He
took from within a faded, threadbare
coat whose appearance betokened the
Sunday garment. Then he stooped,
picked up the coin and slipped it emphatically into a pocket in the coat,

which he laid across a chair. After
this he went again to bed, and slept.

VII.

The congregation were dispersing in
various directions across the square,
chatting with that decorous cordiality
and chastened but relieved expression
that follows a fifty-minute sermon. As
the figure of Parson Knowles came
from the church door, Ezra Spicer, who
had lingered timidly about the vesti-
bule, approached the minister and
taking off his hat spoke a few words
falteringly to him. A knot of men of
Spicer's age and acquaintance, who
were crossing the street into the little
public square, catching sight of the in-
terview, paused and stared in legiti-
mate surprise. Ezra Spicer had been
to church for the first time in months
—he had given to the collection,
for the first time in years, and now as
though to crown this unprecedented be-

havior, he was speaking for the first time in his life with Parson Knowles.

As the two passed slowly to the street from the church steps, and turned in the direction of the parsonage, it was seen that Spicer was speaking, to judge from his nervous gesticulation, with more earnestness than fluency, and that a curious expression, half pity, half amusement, dwelt upon the parson's face.

. . . "So, sir," said Ezra, "I could n't give it back to Carter an' tell what I 'd been. I s'pose I ought to ha' done so, but I somehow could n't do it. An' if I 'd spent it fer myself I 'd been worse 'n Benedick Arnol', an' so I thought I 'd kind o' give it to the plate."

"Well, Ezra," said the parson gently, "it seems to me you 've atoned for what little wrong—no, it was more—it was more—it was a great wrong—but there was strong temptation, and you yielded but a moment after all. I think you 've atoned, and the money will not be missed by Sampson. There are plenty to see that he has all he needs to take him out of danger."

"But you see, sir," Ezra began again, then stopped, looking sheepishly away.

"Well!"

"Why, you see, sir," Spicer went on hurriedly, "I was goin' to tell you before, but I could n't make out to. I give that money jest as if 't was reelly mine. I dropped it in so 's every one could see—like Deacon Stovey does." He stopped, alarmed at his boldness in commenting upon the action of one of the pillars of the church, and looked shyly at the parson. Dr. Knowles's back was turned and he was looking fixedly across Squire Weston's fence towards a barn at the rear of the yard. Mrs. Weston, from a front window, saw, not without a slight sense of scandal, that the good pastor's face was convulsed with most unsabbath-like silent laughter. "Well," said Parson Knowles, after a convulsive but successful effort at self-control, " well, the Squire's old barn looks like new in its fresh coat of paint—and Ezra—I think your ostentation will be forgiven —it's very human—and it's human to err; why, deacons do," he said—with a quick catch in his breath and a gleam in his eyes that surprised Spicer—" and just one thing more, my boy," he said, kindly laying his hand with a gentle touch upon the young man's shoulder, " it would do no harm and it *might* do good, who knows, if you came regularly to church, even though you haven't a single copper for the plate." He turned into his gate as he said this and Ezra, bowing reverently, turned in his homeward direction. As he passed the group of curious spectators, still standing at the edge of the square, various pleasantries assailed him.

" Say, Ezry, is it a fac' that y're goin' to take charge o' the new meetin'-house to South Tiberius?"

"Oh, Ezry, did ye set parson right about that there ninthly o' his 'n?"

"Wal, Ezry, what's yer hurry? Eagle bar aint open Sabbath!"

Proof to these shafts of humor, Ezra held silently upon his way. "I never seen the beat o' that," said one of the group as they strolled across the square. "You'd think he was parson's right hand deacon. And did ye see him drop a dollar in the plate?" "That's what s'prizes me," said another—"give a hull dollar! There was a week's drink in that fer Ezry."—"Give it jist like Deacon Stovey, too," said a third—"held his hand high an' dropped it so's all could see. Ezry must ha' come into prop'ty." The group paused in the centre of the square. A fourth who had not yet expressed an opinion rubbed his chin diffidently and summed up the entire matter. "Wal, ye can't never tell what's goin' to happen! Goin' my way, Issachar?" And the knot resolved itself into its individual strands.

VIII.

The following Sunday Ezra Spicer was again in church. Although his appearance there had not the galvanic effect it had caused the previous Sabbath among his acquaintance, the surprise was distinct, and those who knew him breathed heavily and settled themselves with patience and confidence to await the relapse. Their confidence was not ill-grounded.

The second Sunday from the first herein described was a sultry, overcast day. Flies were in the air—the wild flies of the fields and woods. The trout were leaping in Wolf Run, and no one knew it better than Ezra Spicer.

The church bell was ringing, and from out a side street whither he had gone to visit an ailing friend, Parson Knowles was hastening churchwards. Presently he was aware that a familiar figure bearing rod and creel had rounded a corner a few rods away and was coming towards him. It was Ezra Spicer, and the parson knew that in a moment they would meet. He saw the discomfited fisherman pause, turn round, and linger miserably as though awaiting some one who followed. Pitying the distress of the backslider, and with an instinct as refined as it was compassionate, he turned into the first gateway at hand, followed the sidewalk to the house, and finding the door ajar, knocked and entered.

It was Deacon Stovey's mansion, and that sainted man was about to sally forth to worship. The parson held him a moment in converse, and presently Ezra drifted furtively but swiftly by. The Deacon saw him through a hall window. "There," he said, "I did n't calkilate *he 'd* keep up church goin' long! Goin' to Wolf Run, *I 'll* warrant." —"Well," said the parson reflectively, "you know some people worship better in the fields and woods."

"Yes, but parson," said the deacon

irascibly, "he need n't be a-fishin',
too."

"Why, St. Peter was a fisherman,"
said Parson Knowles merrily, and the
reply silenced the deacon, although the
comparison invoked was not in all ways
a close one.

The Case of Pinckney Tolliver.

157

The Case of Pinckney Tolliver.

WOLF RUN is not tributary to the river. While the other brooks of the vicinity swell the voice of the stream, piping treble of the sixth age compared to its once sonorous tone, Wolf Run, from a higher level, holds a winding course to a deep lake whose broad expanse terminates a valley to the west of Dorset.

In this brook the trout yet find an abiding place. The undergrowth is still rank about the feeding springs, and saw-mills have not defiled the cool runnels with their piny refuse. Under alders, under willows, slow and deep where elm and buttonwood throw their shade, swift and shallow through sunny pasture land, discoursing noisily to half-sunken fallen trees whose water-logged branches have bred dams and miniature cataracts, Wolf Run seeks the answer to its twelve-mile questioning in the cool heart of the lake.

Along the brook, one midday in early June, I wandered, now picking a trout from a quiet hole by aid of the humble earthworm, again with " brown hackle " tossing upon a riffle deceiving some more athletic fish as he lay watching the swift water. I thought in the morning it would rain ; at noon I was sure of it, and more than casual acquaintance with the thunder-storm brewed among the Pulteney hills, warned me that the rain, though perhaps brief, would be drenching. With this thought in mind I had lingered, as the sky grew darker, in the neighborhood of an ancient gambrel-roofed barn, situated in a pasture lot through one corner of which the brook ran. The barn had been red in its prime, but stress of weather and flight of time had tarnished, and dimmed and the sides showed streaks and patches of gray. The great doors opened east and west and two sheds formed with the main structure three sides of a quadrangle. It was one of those mighty barns which have about them an air of grandeur as though conscious of being the trusted repository of the riches inherited from man's natural benefactress and common mother.

There was a house not distant. It was neither distinctive nor impressive, and I felt sure its owner in describing his premises would say, " The *house* is not far from the barn."

While making a mental inventory of the neighborhood a flash, followed by a rumble, caused me to reel hastily in, adjust my creel and scramble over the worm-fence which separated me from the pasture lot. I made quick way to the barn and reached it just as the first big drops rattled upon its roof.

The broad east door was wide open,

showing against a dusky background, a
fanning-machine, a democrat wagon
and a row of portly oat sacks. Upon
these sacks sat two young men, either
of whom might have been twenty-five
years of age, while upon a keg and near
the wagon whose wheels were several
inches deep in hay-dust, was seated an
oldish man in faded overalls. A man
of spare but powerful frame and a
countenance at once weather-beaten,
wrinkled and youthful. He was en-
gaged in the tranquilizing business of
whittling a potato, and favoring his
occupation with an accompaniment of
discourse.

As I approached the barn-door, dis-
turbing a gathering of fowls that had
clustered about it and that commented
variously upon my sudden appearance,
the man with the potato paused in the
midst of his remarks. He looked at
me a moment amiably but impassively
as though I were an ordinary conse-
quence of a thunder-shower, then re-

sumed the interrupted flow of his words. His face, I fancied, showed signs of satisfaction at the increase in his audience, for I at once settled myself to listen, taking a place beside the younger men who with friendly glances made room for me.

"So I don't never vote the demercratic ticket unless,"—here the speaker paused for at least a quarter of a minute, looking with mild curiosity into my creel, the cover of which had flapped open—"unless I happen to take a mind to."

At this proof of conversational stratagem, the original auditors laughed with a sort of diffident enjoyment and looked to me for encouragment. I was aware of the presence of one of those characters found upon American countrysides who unite in equal proportions the virtues of sage, philosopher, and humorist, and I gave token of my appreciation.

"Yes," said the whittler, harking back

163

to a story which I had not heard and did not understand, but which had seemed to its narrator of sufficient merit to entitle it to a semi-resuscitation,—"Yes," he repeated, "as we come to the ditch, there sat the gen'er'l an' his staff. They was to wind of us, an' I sez to the boys, 'Boys' I sez, 'they's a *still* around here somewhar', sez I." Again the young rustics laughed, and I laughed too.

"You were in the war?" I asked presently, as the speaker was silent a moment over his whittling.

"Wal, yes, fer a little spell I was," he answered; "went out with Cap'n John Denison's Comp'ny—know him? Wal, no; you could n' hardly know him. He was killed, to Gaines Mills, when you must ha' been perty young."

"Yes," I answered, "I was pretty young then. John Denison, though, was my mother's cousin."

"Was, hay! Then who be you?"

This interrogation, peremptory as it may appear in print, in the slow drawl of the old farmer was perfectly civil, and I answered it as fully as seemed necessary.

" Why, I knew yer pa when he was younger 'n you be now. Knowed him 'fore *you* did, I guess." The audience, myself included, acknowledged the drollery.

" Yes *sir;* I knew yer pa 'fore he went to the city. He was a handsome young feller as you want to see. Somehow you don't look like yer pa to me."

This observation following so closely upon the tribute to my father's comeliness embodied a comment unfavorable but unintentional, and speaker and audience were aware of it. Amusement was predominant with me; the two young farmers were also suppressing smiles, whilst the older man was obviously concerned at what he had unconsciously implied and without looking up redoubled his attention to the potato, now about the size of a pigeon's egg.

"Wal," he said presently, "I s'pose likely you took after yer ma."

At this sad attempt at bettering matters I laughed outright, to the relief of the two younger men who heartily joined. Had the cause of this mirth been an Irishman he would even then have extricated himself from his tangle, but being a Pulteney County Yankee, he merely reddened, smiled sheepishly, and getting up, strolled to the door and gazed upon the weather.

"Rainin' agin," he said presently, willing to change the topic but averse to losing control of the conversation. "'Rainin' agin like a dern fool,' as ole Deacon Adams said when it showered in hayin'. Wal, wal, so you 're the Judge's son, be ye?" Having rounded the troublesome corner he was again upon the original track.

"Why, I was on the jury 'n the first case, pretty nigh, yer pa ever tried. He wa'n't so old as Lemuel there, by four year. Gosh all hemlock, thet *was* a dern amusin' case." Here the speaker paused and turning his eyes full of reminiscent dreaminess upon my face inquired with perfect recklessness of the effect of double negatives. "Didn't he never tell ye 'bout the ' Pink Tolliver ' law case ? "

I replied that while I recalled some mention by my father of complications in the life of one Pinckney Tolliver, the matter was not familiar to me, and that I was eager to hear the details from one who doubtless knew them well, and had weighed them with the impartiality of a juror. I was so urgent in my request that after a moment spent in gazing pensively upon the barn-floor and choking back what was evidently a rising tide of merriment, he complied.

"You see," he began, "ole Pink Tolliver, Susan's husband, was livin' clost to Elder Rice's back line. (You know the ole Rice house in Dorset ?) Wal,

just to rear was a lane full of colored
folks, an' they was plenty in Dorset
forty year back. Next to Elder Rice
Cap'n Weston had his house an' printin'
office to once. Now they wa'n't no
nicer woman, 'cordin to my notion, in
all Dorset, black or white, than Aunt
Susan Tolliver, but Pink was never
himself out o' jail. First place he was
allus drunk, an' nex' place it didn't seem
natch'l to be loose. Pink was a thief as
well as a sot ; anyhow he stole chickens.
Gen'u'lly he went up town fer his
thievin'—had too much sense to steal
clost to home ; an' then the Rices an'
ole Cap'n Weston had been good to
Susan, an' I s'pose Pink had a kind o'
colored sense o' gratitude, or, mebbe
Susan made him keep his hands off
their fowls. He had once got away
with one o' Cap'n Weston's duckwing
games, but he swore he jess borryed it
fer a fight an' the chicken got hurt ac-
cidentally an' died, an' he s'posed the
Cap'n would't care fer the corpse, so

the Tollivers eat him. That was Pink's
account, I reck'lect. Wal, one night
Pink got tangle-foot enough to kind o'
mix him up an' make him fergetful, an'
nex' day two fine dominicks ole Mis'
Rice was braggin' 'bout puttin' in the
fair, was missin'. 'Spishun an' footprints an' feathers an' word o' mouth o'
young Joe Macy who seen Pink carryin' 'em over Elder's fence, pinted pretty
straight to the Tolliver shanty. Ole
Elder was kind o' pervoked—ye see he
jess ben helpin' Pink an' his fam'ly
through a bad winter,—an' he allowed
Pink could go up for a few months an'
live on the county. So they 'rested
him an' brought him to trial. I d' know
now why Pink didn't plead guilty,
'nless 't was he felt sure o' conviction
an' kind o' enjoyed bein' notorious;
but he pleaded not guilty an' Judge
Caldwell, Pink havin' no cash fer lawyers, appointed yer pa to defend him.

"'No money in it my young friend,'
sez the Judge, 'but they *is* some glory,

169

ef you acquit Pinckney in the face of
appearances,' sez he, an' Pink he grinned
all over, jest tickled with his prominence.

"Wal, yer pa was younger 'n what he
is now, leastways 'cording to my figur-
in', an' he took up the case fer all it was
worth. I was on the jury an' so was
ole Cap'n Weston. 'Bijah Sears from
South Tiberius-way was prosecutin'
attorney an' he said lots 'bout yer pa
bein' so young. It was, 'Oh, baby, do
ye think so?' an' 'Is that so, baby?'
an', 'Why, baby, I was practisin' law
when you was cuttin' teeth, an' ye haint
cut 'em all yet, I guess'—an' all sich
talk. 'T want right—I said so to Cap'n
Weston, an' ole Cap'n he sez to me:
'You hold your hosses, Sam,' he sez;
'the boy kin wrastle him, leave him
alone.'

"Wal, yer pa was pretty mad, an'
when he got good an' goin', he give
'Bijah jessy, an' he give it to him hot.
'Mebbe I *haint* cut all my teeth yit,' sez

170

he. ' I'm only twenty-one I admit,' sez
he, ' but,' he sez, ' what does this here
jury think of a man what 's got to be
sixty year old an' more an' haint never
cut a *wisdom* tooth yit—no, nor aint
like to, to jedge from appearances,' sez
he."

Here the narrator paused a moment,
slapping his knee and laughing with a
laugh that seemed to begin upon the
exterior of his physiognomy and work
slowly in. The last chuckle swallowed,
and a bit of encouragment derived from
his amused and interested audience, he
went on.

"Wall, that took the crowd, an'
Pink he laffed too,—the ole nigger
allus liked the boys,—an' Marcellus
Jones from Mileyville, who was into
court that day, jess lay back on the
winder-sill an' laffed an' cussed—they
called him swearin' Marce Jones—till
the Judge said he 'd clear the court.
' Good fer baby ! ' says Marce, an'
cussed an' ripped an' cussed, ' baby kin

wrastle ye, 'Bijy Sears!' Yes, sir, the Judge had to stop him, an' the Judge he was laffin' too. 'Gentlemen,' sez he —I allus liked Judge Caldwell's way o' speakin'—'Gentlemen, this here case don't rest on priority o' practice, or sen'ority of age,' sez he, an' yer pa went on. I can't think of all he said, ner what 'Bijy said back, but yer pa made a hot fight. Still the evidence was too heavy fer Pink.

"'The feathers *might* ha' blown into the Tolliver yard, as baby sez,' sez 'Bijy, 'but there haint no wind in Pulteney County high 'nuff to blow into Mr. Rice's yard footprints the size o' them I measured Monday last, leadin' from the premises o' the plaintiff's fowls to the defendant's fence. Them footprints was Pinckney Tolliver's, gentlemen o' the jury, an' they can't be matched fer size 'tween here an' the Pennsylvany line.'

"Wall, this was a pint fer 'Bijy's side, an' every one, purty nigh, laffed, an'

the hull case was spiled by Pink, who
was three parts drunk, sayin' ' dat 's so
boss, dat 's so ; ' he was so dern puffed
up by what 'Bijy sez. Yer pa, he never
would ha' taken the case only the
judge appinted him, tried to shet Tolliver up, but the cat was loose an' they
wan't no need o' young Joe Macy's
testimony hardly at all ; an' the case
went to the jury.

  " Wal, Cap'n Weston allus had a likin'
fer yer pa—used to get him to write
editorials fer his paper, *The Dorset Patriot*, when he was n't to home himself,
an' he 'd listened to the summin' up
fer the defense, all ears. Every now
an' then he 'd chuckle or grunt, never
takin' his eyes off yer pa. When we
got into the jury-room Caleb Cooper,
ole Major's nephew, scz, ' I guess they
aint no doubt 'bout Pink's guilt.'

  " I sez ' no,' an' most the others sez
' guess not ' or somethin', meanin' the
same. Ole Cap'n Weston spoke up—
' I *dunno*,' he sez, ' I *dunno*.'

"'You dunno?' says Caleb. 'Did ye follow the trial?' He was a whig an' Cap'n was a demercrat an' they wan't no love lost 'tween 'em.

"'Yes I did,' says Cap'n, 'yes I *did* sir,' sez he, 'an' *I* did n't find no time fer nappin,' sez he. Wal, Caleb had kind o' closed his eyes a spell an' so he shet up, but Deacon Edwards sez:

"'W'y Cyrus,' he sez, 'you know Pink's a thievin' vagabond anyhow; he stole your chickins once. I hearn ye tell on it.'

"'Stole one chickin' from me, to be exact,' says ole Cap'n, 'one duckwing game rooster to match agin Cato Watson's brown red. 'T want a good fight; the duckwing run, after a little, an' I disowned him, leastways I would ef I 'd known he showed mongrel; an' Pink was welcome to him.

"Wal, the deacon did n't see jess how the duckwing showin' yaller dog went to provin' Pink was n't a thief an' he said so, but ole Cap'n he kept on argy-

174

fyin' and talkin'. Bime-by he got Selah
Ruggles an' Alpheus Taylor onto a
religious discussion an' half the jury
takin' sides, an' when that blew over
an' we was takin' a ballot 'bout half-
past six in the evenin,' he said he
'bleeved some of the evidence wa'n't
properly interduced.

" ' Wa'n't, hay ? ' says Caleb Cooper,
' wal, I 'm a good 'nuff lawyer to know
it was, every word of it sir,' sez he.

" ' You 're a lawyer, be ye,' sez
Cap'n—' You 're a lawyer, hay ? Wal, I
thought you called yourself an editor,
but ef you 're a lawyer what call have
you sittin' on a jury ? ' sez he.

" ' I said lawyer enough, sir,' sez
Caleb.

" ' Yes,' sez Cap'n, ' an' you 've said
most everything cnough, an' perhaps a
leetle mite too much, 'specially in yer
newspaper,' sez he.

" Wal this het up Caleb, an' first we
knew we had all the learnin' from
the back files o' the *Patriot* an' the

Freeman fer six months an' mebbe a year. It was eight o'clock 'fore we got another ballot an' Cap'n Weston voted 'no' agin, an' the only 'no,' like it was before. We all kep' at him fer a spell an' he promised to think the hull thing over ef we 'd leave him in peace, so he went into a corner an' smoked an' the rest of us sat round an' felt hungry, 'cept Selah Ruggles an' Alpheus. They dug up the hatchet agin an' we might ha' known what 'ud come of it. 'Bout nine o'clock we asked Cap'n ef his mind wan 't satisfied an' he sez, 'how kin I think with Selah an' elder Taylor, talkin', talkin' brilliantly too,' he sez, chucklin' to himself, ' on subjec's so much more important. An' we got no ballot.

"Wal 'bout nine-thirty he riz up an' sez to Alpheus that a great light had come upon his mind an' he believed Pink really stole them dominick pullets.

"It did n't take long to get a-ballotin', an' 'bout ten, the court-house bell rang

176

to say we had reached a verdic'. They was quite a crowd come in. Every one expected a verdic' in half an hour, an' when we stayed out till ten, from half-past five in the afternoon, they was a lot who felt kind o' curious.

"I see yer pa come in. He looked contented, 's much 's to say, 'fer an open an' shet thing I give 'em somethin' to chaw on.' An' there was 'Bijy a-lookin' a little anxious, an' Pink too, an' he seemed kind o' scared an' disappinted; you see he sot store by jail life, Pink did.

"Of course the verdic' suited every one, Tolliver, most of all, an' the crowd bust up. I see Cap'n Weston shake hands with yer pa an' walk off with him; they was laffin' together. Next day I met the Cap'n an' I sez, 'Cap'n,' I sez, 'you an' me 's both demercrats an' I take yer newspaper, an' I want you to do me a favor, I sez.'

"'Wal, Sam,' sez he, 'what is it?'

"'Wal,' I sez, 'you pass fer a

pretty smart man. What 'n the land's
name made ye doubt Pink took them
pullets, fer five long dry hours,' sez I.
   " ' Doubt it,' sez he, ' I *never* doubted
it; why Sam,' sez he, ' I seen him as
well as Joe Macy. I was up with my
youngest child an' heard the noise, an'
seen Pink climb the fence with them
dominicks. But I wan't goin' to have
that boy beat in his fust case without a
big fight in the jury-room,' sez he.
' He 's as likely a young man as you
want to see anywhere, an' I wan't goin'
to have no lightnin' verdic' mortifyin'
him right at the start.' "
   The narrator paused. His anecdote
was obviously at an end and I showed
due appreciation of his reminiscent
gifts. The sun was shining once more,
and bidding good-day to the young
countrymen, who had, from being quite
in touch with me, during the foregoing
narration, relapsed into diffidence again,
I took my rod and creel and left the
shelter of the barn. As I passed the

threshold, my friend the philosopho-humorist, who had come to the door of the barn, accosted me :

"See that stump-field yonder? Wal, I took 'bout thirty-five nice trout down there, one Sabbath mornin' in '53, 'fore breakfast. I don't know if they be any there now. I s'pose I would n't fish now on the Sabbath day unless," here he paused and looked dreamily at me for almost a quarter of a minute, " unless I was sure o' gettin' a nice mess."

The Last of the Old Church.

The Last of the Old Church.

THE doors of the old church stood wide open though the day was not the Sabbath. The morning wind, still cool and grateful to trees rusty with the dust of midsummer, sent reckless draughts chasing each other along the aisles, and whirling the leaves of a few tattered hymnals, not yet taken from the church. A light dust came from the open windows occasioned by the removal of the pews, as one by one these time-honored seats were brought into the open air and huddled together in front of the doors.

For the "old church" of Dorset was to be levelled to the ground.

Seventy years it had stood, on the

south side of the shady village square, fronting one of the main streets, gazing benignly upon the growth of the town whose sons were, many of them, its god-children. For a long time it had been the only place of worship in Dorset, and as such had been sufficient unto the needs of the townspeople. But with the railroad came increase in population, and diversity in sect; several spires now peered from among the village elms and maples, and the congregation of the old church voted almost unanimously, to pull down and build greater.

The word *unanimously* might have been proper, had it not been for the stubborn opposition of Major Cooper. He regarded the enterprise as conceived in folly, and ending in sacrilege. He was a remnant of old Dorset. He had seen the town enter and emerge from its teens, and he was willing and indeed desirous as he stated in his elaborate minority report, delivered orally upon

every street corner and at frequent intervals, to rescue the younger genera-
tion from such a piece of irreverence.
The other members of the congregation refused, however, to be saved by
the remnant, and it so happened that on
a morning of middle August the noise of
shingles wrenched from their place, and
clattering to the ground, disturbed the
usually quiet neighborhood of the old
church ; attracting, as the day wore on,
a knot of idle and curious townspeople.

At ten o'clock Major Cooper came
into view from the direction of the
" Eagle " tavern.

" Came into view " is strictly the
phrase to employ regarding the advent
of Major Cooper. He never broke
upon the sight with the unseemly pre-
cipitation of a man who had business
and no rheumatism. His approach was
always gradual and full of the benignity
of Indian Summer. Upon this particular morning his coming was attended by
an air of unusual dignity, and the spec-

tators left staring at the dismantlement of the church to look at the white-haired old man as he advanced. His opposition to the new church was well known, and so vigorously had he voiced his sentiments, that it seemed not improbable that some new burst of eloquence might add a zest to the morning's entertainment.

But Major Cooper was beyond words. Heeding none of the greetings offered him as he entered the group of idlers, he went to the array of pews and looked long and earnestly among them. At last he laid hold of one, upon whose back some boy's work, an initial or monogram, caught his eye. It was his own pew, and bore the handiwork of the first Barlow knife of his boyhood. With much exertion the old man dragged the heavy seat from out the huddle of pews to the edge of the street. One of the onlookers came forward and offered a hand.

" Don't you touch it, don't you touch

it, Balcom," panted the Major angrily, "you can run the church, you boys. I 'll run my pew for a while longer, anyway."

Balcom retired in some confusion and Major Cooper slowly and amid much dust dragged his old pew across the street and under the shade of a maple. Then he sat down in it, wedged himself into a corner, and wiping his face of the sweat of unusual exertion, proceeded to contemplate the work of destruction.

In the old church, with its white-washed pillars, its gleaming steeple, its green blinds and square-paned windows, were for him the peculiarly consecrated associations of a life-time. There he had been baptized, there, too, had his brothers and sisters been named; from the pulpit were uttered the words of his father's funeral sermon, and before that pulpit he himself would have been married. Old bachelor though he was, he could not forget what ought to have

187

been, what might have been, and where
it would have been. Baptisms, mar-
riages, deaths, the recollections that
stand aloof and peculiar in the land of
memory, were represented to him by
the old church.

The shingles, split and wrenched
from the nails, rattled noisily upon the
ground. The Major gripped his cane
in gusty indignation. It seemed to him
as though some one were tearing leaves
from his family Bible.

Now during this time the only other
individual to whom the razing of the
church was a particular offense, was
seated by the river a quarter of a mile
away, upon a green rib of bank, angling
pensively. His location commanded
an excellent view of the old church, and
from time to time Ezra gazed fixedly
in its direction. Each glance was dis-
approved by a slow shake of the head.

It was not usual with Ezra Spicer to
fish "Denison's Hole" of a week day.
It was his Sunday fishing-ground. For

many years it had been to the old man's
quaint mind an alleviation of conscience
to fish within sight of the church. Sometimes through its open windows, on a
favoring wind, the " Portuguese " hymn
or " Federal Street " drifted across Cooper's meadows and joined the natural
music of the Connedaga. On Sundays,
too, Ezra condemned himself to fish for
mullets, this fish being particularly diffi-
cult to capture. As men who do not
smoke sometimes love to hold an un-
lighted cigar between their teeth, so
Ezra Spicer of a Sunday dropped into
the water a hook upon which he hardly
expected a fish to fasten himself. In
this way he felt that some sort of treaty
had been compounded with the divine
powers supposed to be hostile to Sunday fishing. He had chosen " Denison's Hole " this day, though it was
Thursday, for its location.

Across the fields, distinct against the
green of the little square, Ezra watched
the church, swarmed over by gangs of

workmen, and his keen eyes took stock as well of the figure of Major Cooper, rigid and uncompromising, in one corner of his family pew. The fisherman chuckled furtively. "Ol' Maj.," he said to himself, "Ol' Maj.!" and wagged his head. Presently he lifted a catfish upon the bank, pricked his finger while taking it from the hook, and indulged in a little home-made expletive. He was aware of no scruple regulating the use of the genuine article of profanity, but he belonged to that class of weak characters who swear usually only upon parade, and in the presence of those apt to be impressed by wholesale breakage of the commandment. By himself he used phrases in accord with his surroundings, woody forest expletives, raucous and vigorous and entailing technically no penalty.

"Crotch all hemlock," said he, putting his thumb to his mouth. "Slab-sided, basswood bullhead ye! Like ol' Major," he added, chuckling again,

'mean to handle when he 's mad, an'
hang on to things like a pup to a root."
Aphorisms touching the mental and
physical aspects of young canines in
certain emergencies were rife in Ezra's
repertory. "Wal, I d' know as I kin
blame 'im," he continued, "town aint
nowhere nigh so pious as 't was, an' yit
they must have a new meetin'-house."
Then, after a pause, he drew his line
again from the water, wound it around
the pole, picked up his tin pail half
filled with catfish and chub and rambled slowly along the bank. "Guess
I 'll go over an' take a look at things,
if water aint too deep on the riffle," he
muttered.

It was an easy thing, stepping from
stone to stone, to cross the Connedaga,
dryfoot, at the long reach of swift
water below the Cooper meadows, and
having traversed the fields Ezra presently found himself in a lane at the
side of the church. The clapboards, by
this time, were partly gone from its

walls, and the old man peered, with curiosity mixed with awe, into the building. Through many gaps in the roof and sides the sunlight gazed wantonly ; light used for several generations to enter decorously by the open door or through the great square windows.

"Hold on a minute, Ezry," shouted a workman from the roof, "we 'll show ye in a minute what th' inside of a church looks like,—that 'll be a kind o' s'prize fer ye." Several others amplified this sally, but it had no effect upon the old man. Heedless of witticism he pushed his way among the idlers about the building, passed the loitering boys in the street in front, and finally stopped before the white-haired Major, who still glowered from the corner of his pew. For a time neither spoke ; then the Major, as though continuing a conversation already some time under way, said :

" 'T aint good enough for 'em Ezry, 't aint good enough for 'em."

"Good enough for me," he went on
bitterly, " good enough for my father
and old Parson Knowles an' the others
up there." He waved his cane in
the direction of the burying-ground.
"Sit down, Ezry," he added with a
friendly glance at the other ancient,
" my pew's about all that will be left
pretty soon of the old church. Sit
down, let's do a little preachin'—better
sit down," he reiterated, "you 're not
in very good standin', you know."
Ezra chuckled softly, laid his rod and
pail by the side of the old oaken seat,
and sat gingerly down.

"We 're gettin' old, you an' me," he
ventured, terminating a long pause.
The Major started from a reverie.

" What 's that ? " he said.

" We 're gettin' old you an' me," repeated the other.

" I 've got ten years older since mornin'," said the Major, huskily. "I 'm
losin' part of my memory, right there,
with those old beams. I never went

inside the old place but I saw corners, or pews, yes, or stains on the walls to make me laugh at what they brought up, or feel like cryin'. Look yonder at that spot on the gallery wall. Know who sat there? Cap'n Riddle, for years out o' mind."

Across the church, upon the wall, plainly visible, in the light pouring into the roofless room, was a blurred dusky blotch. It was there that the town-crier, who was also a blacksmith, and at times performed riotously upon a bass drum, rested his head during service— Captain Riddle. Captain by reason of a manner that suggested freely the pomp and circumstance of war. Him had the village genius when a lad, apostrophized in an heroic stanza beginning :

" Captain Riddle, son of Mars,
    Reared amid the battle smoke,"

and ending with the pertinent query,

" Why, oh why, from over eatin'
    Will you go to sleep in meetin' ?"

"Wal, Cap'n's gone, too," said Ezra, gloomily. "He was a man I liked. Now, Deacon Stovey I never could stand; used to pass plate, an' then turn round to the people an' drop in a dollar —just to show how pious and generous he was ; did it every Sunday for years."

"Every Sunday, hay," said the Major enquiringly. "I suppose you saw him, Ezry?"

Ezra blushed. "Wal," he said, "he did *once*, for I seen him, an' my wife she told me 'bout the other spells. Tell ye Major," he added, "I may not hev ben quite so regular as you was to church, but I seen a sight there one day you missed ; you was to Albany, I recklect. You see, ol' Scott, Cap'n Weston's dog, got tired o' listenin' to sermon that day—some new man from out o' town was preachin'. Scott was pretty well behaved in church, but they was somethin' he did n't take to in this new preacher. Wal, you remember he gen'ly slep' close to the pulpit steps ;

he got up 'bout half through sermon, looked round the church a minute, then gave one o' them long yawns a dog *will* give, 's if he was snappin' at the last end of a squeak. You know what I mean. Wal, Jimmy Barton laughed right out, allus laughed on half a chance, that boy, an' Deacon Stovey comes out o' his pew and kicks poor Scott into the aisle. Cap'n Weston runs out and ketches hold o' Deacon. ' You kickin' my dog,' sez he to Deacon ? ' Don't you see I be ?' sez Deacon. ' Wal, I 'll do my own dog-kickin'' sez Cap'n, 'an' I 'll do it work-days' sez he. ' Now they 's some *men* that's mean enough fer ye to break the Sabbath to kick 'em." he sez, lookin' Deacon over. Wal, Deacon wa' nt no match fer Cap'n, an' he went an' sat down ; but it wa'nt ten days 'fore that story 'bout the Weston's havin' pie for breakfast come out an' come from ol' Mis' Stovey too."

The Major was laughing heartily as

Ezra ceased speaking—a genial reminiscent laugh. For a time he forgot the personal and present grievance of the church's destruction, and bringing an old smooth worn silver box from his pocket, helped himself and handed the box to Spicer.

"Well, well," he said presently. "I remember hearing about that at the time. An' the pie scandal! Why it bred a quarrel that lasted years. Were you at church the day young Parson Hawley from South Tiberius preached?"

Ezra pondered with the air of one to whom the past was such a wilderness of attendances upon divine worship that to locate one particular occasion was a work of hopeless magnitude. "I think mullets was runnin', 'bout then," he said at last with a shy chuckle.

"Well," said the Major, "you know the whole story of course as well as I do," and disregarding the fact that Ezra admitted a full acquaintance with

its features he proceeded to detail them
with much exactness. One of the
notable characteristics of the good
Major was his infinite zest in the repe-
tition of anecdote. The more threadbare it grew, the more it was endeared
to him; and his joyous smile at the
right moment, and the artless way in
which he looked around his audience
for appreciation, disarmed possible
criticism.

"You see," he began, "Parson
Knowles was filling a pulpit for a Sunday, down Tioga way, somewhere, an'
Cap'n Weston got young Hawley
from South Tiberius to come over to
fill the vacancy. Rather a bright boy,
young Hawley—just out of college, an'
knew almost half as much as he
thought he did, an' that 's sayin' a good
deal. He was pretty often up to
Weston's and people said it was a
match 'tween Eunice Weston an' him.
Well, it was about ten months after
Mrs. Deacon Stovey put the dictionary

on a stool an' the stool on a table an'
looked through *her* window across an'
through the Weston's—the day she says
she saw 'em have pie for breakfast.
Guess that story was a fact. Why,
old Cap'n never denied it. 'Major'
says he, when the story came out—'I
eat pie when I like, an' I like—most
every chance that comes my way,' says
he laughin'. 'T was Eunice an' Sally
an' Mrs. Weston made the noise.
Well, as I was sayin,' 't was perhaps ten
months after the pie disclosure an'
everything was pretty hot yet. Young
Hawley gave out as his text that
Sabbath in church, that verse from
Romans, 'For one believeth that he
may eat all things, another who is weak
eateth herbs.'

"Well, no one thought anything
'bout that bein' a specially pat text,
until young Jimmy Barton turned
round to John Denison just back of
him, an' says loud enough for half the
church to hear, 'an' some eat pie for

breakfast!' Well, 't want any use—the congregation came down, an' Cap'n Weston laughed too, but Mrs. Weston an' Sally an' Eunice. Well!

"I saw Hawley eatin' Sunday dinner alone that day, at the tavern, an' I reck'lect seein' Jimmy an' young Joe Weston rough-an'-tumblin', next day in front the school-house. Now that Jimmy was a takin' boy!"

"He was so, he was so," agreed Ezra with enthusiasm. I learnt Jim to fish, him an' Homer Silsbee,—an' we knew the river better 'n some folks knows their prayers. Now ol' Judge Barton——"

"Old Judge Barton was a *leetle* bit too severe with Jimmy," resumed the Major, taking the conversation again in hand, as one driving takes up the reins laid down a moment. "He was proud of the boy, but he did n't quite make him out. You see the Judge was all New England, and Mrs. Barton was half Scotch. There was the Judge's

pew yonder, where they're rippin' up
the floor. Who's bossin' that job?
Steve Morgan, hay! Why look at that
now—look at that! He never came to
church once in six months, that fellow
—never belonged—wouldn't have been
tolerated—been a drunkard—beats his
wife—been in jail—an' look at him
there, tearin' up the floor he wasn't fit
to walk upon, damn him!"

The Major, tremulous with rage, had
fallen back into an army habit, which
he discountenanced in others and usually steered clear of himself. The slip
brought him to a pause, and he turned
with a deprecating smile towards Ezra.
He observed a depressed expression
upon the latter's face.

"Well," he said, "a man can take a
drink once in a while, Ezry, of course,
an' no great harm—do myself. We'll
stop at the 'Eagle' as we go down
town ; an' not attendin' service regularly 's no crime, but you see, Steve
Morgan, that——. Well, well, I'll not

let loose again. That's where the Judge's seat was, an' Elder Rhodes just in front. You remember old Madam Denison's sister, Miss Caldwell? Of course you do. She wore more hoop-skirt than any woman ever I saw. One Sunday, you were n't there —trout risin' I believe—she came in late. Elder Rhodes's tile-hat was just outside his pew and the swirl of her skirts just hauled it right in like a cob into the feeder. Out jumps Elder an' follows up the aisle, duckin' down each step an' reachin' for his hat. But he never got it till Miss Caldwell sat down. Oh, how Johnny Denison, an' Jim Barton, an' a raft of young ones laughed. So did Mrs. Barton, but the Judge never smiled. You know he had a square pew with a table in it. Jim sat next the aisle that day, then his three sisters, then the Judge. They were singin' the second hymn, 'Duke Street,' I think it was, an' the Judge never looked up from his book. He located Jim by instinct, an' took him by the ear—then he marched him north along one side the table, west along the front, south along the other side, an' sat him down 'tween Mrs. Barton an' himself, where Jim would be more convenient, an' never stopped singin' a minute, nor looked up, nor smiled! By the lord Harry," laughed the Major, overcome by the drollery of the recollection and his own humor in relating it, "I don't know now which was the funnier sight, Elder Rhodes rescuing his hat, or Judge Barton suppressing Jimmy!"

"Who sat back of the Bartons, Major? Oh, yes, the Denisons, then come the Callanders, wa'n't it? An' you sat where ye could see the Callanders."

Ezra's diffident chuckle met no response from the other. Major Cooper did not permit even acquaintances from his own walk in life to jest with him on certain subjects, and Ezra had taken a liberty, as he himself recognized. He fumbled with his fish-pole, and yawned several times elaborately, testifying embarrassment in much the manner of a dog who has mingled somewhat in human society. The Major leaned back in his corner, and withdrew into himself, an operation beginning with the retirement of his chin almost wholly within his copious collar.

"Yes," he said presently, with vague stiffness of manner, "I believe I could see the Callander pew from where I sat."

Not only could the Major see the family pew of the Callanders, but he did see it, Sunday after Sunday, year in and out. It held what was more to him than anything else in the little town, where his "all" was to be found. He used to gaze across the church, openly during singing or sermon, furtively in prayer time, at Mrs. Colonel Callander—so beautiful, so beyond him, and to him only a name—a name to a romance closed and laid away upon the shelf of the years. When at last she sat there no longer; when her long widowhood was ended, and she was laid beside her husband, the Major still looked every Sunday across the church to the empty corner in the Callander pew. It took no conjurer's art to tenant it again for him as of old. And sometimes he would suddenly sit straight in his seat, adjust his collar, tug surreptitiously at his coat, and glance quickly towards the other aisle of the church, as if in very truth he felt the eyes of his old time and only love upon him.

The snow that invaded the Major's hair, never touched his heart; there was a green spot there, though it marked the grave of his one passion.

. . . . . .

"Wal, Major, its 'bout noonin'," suggested Ezra, after a long silence. There was no reply.

The old man leaned forward and looked curiously at the Major. He was asleep. The heat of the day, the sudden cessation of the noise about him at the

noon hour, the quiet nature of his recent thoughts, all played a part in the
conspiracy of drowsiness. Ezra muttered discontentedly and looked wist-
fully down the road. He made a movement towards awakening his old friend
but checked himself. A certain irasci-
bility attended upon Major Cooper at
times that deserved and received recognition. So Ezra rose slowly, yawned
loudly, stretched himself, clinked his
rod noisily against the fish-pail and
looked again at the sleeper. The Major
slumbered as deeply as a child. With
a shake of his head Spicer began his
homeward walk, with now and then an
unrewarded backward glance towards
the pew. It was a hot day and the air
was filled with dust. When Ezra had
reached the " Eagle " tavern his natural
aridity was trebled. He sat down for a
few moments upon the steps of the
hostelry. From within he heard a pleas-
ant clink of glasses, and sometimes the
rush of beer from the spigot. He

looked up the road to where the Major still dreamed of other men and other days, and felt a keen sense of deprivation and wrong.

"He asked me to," he muttered, referring to the invitation to refreshment half an hour before, "He asked me to, an' then goes to sleep—'t aint right, that 's what 't aint."

He stooped, picked up his rod and pail, and resumed his way. At the next corner he met Thorne Cooper, the Major's nephew.

"Been fishin', Ezra?" asked Thorne, pleasantly. "No, be'n chasin' a bee swarm," returned the old man sarcastically, pointing to his tackle. Thorne laughed. "Well, I allow I might have known by what you 're carryin'," he said, and passed on.

"Be'n to church, too," called Ezra; "sat in your fam'ly pew. I 'm gettin' high toned. Say, Thorne, jest wake the Major up, will ye? I 'm 'fraid he 'll catch cold sleepin' in the shade.

"There," he chuckled as Cooper went
on up the street, " I 'll just go back to
the ' Eagle ' an let that drink ketch up
to me. Oh, I ain't so *awful* slow."

But as he stopped again by the tavern
door, and watched the figure of Thorne
Cooper nearing the old oak seat under
the maple, a feeling of shame came
over him. He had been the Major's
debtor so often for this or that; for
meat how often, and how very often for
drink. Let the old man sleep his sleep
out!

He jumped up briskly, for his seventy-
odd years, and trotted up the road.

" Thorne—Thorne! " he cried.

The dust was thick, and his voice not
over strong.

He quickened his pace towards the
square, a curious feeling possessing him
that he *must* check his old friend's
awakening.

" Thorne, Thorne! " he called again,
then lessened his pace, for he saw that
Cooper was at the Major's side. He

saw him stoop, touch the old man upon the arm, then shake him gently. He was near enough now to hear his loud exclamation as he bent his head towards his uncle's face.

Major Cooper did not waken. He was to sleep his sleep out, despite all earthly interruptions. The over-exertion of the morning—his struggle with the heavy pew—and the heat of the day, and perhaps one of those sudden ailments always in call of five and seventy years, had closed the old man's eyes forever.

And from the corner-seat in his time-honored pew, in sight of the pulpit that, uncovered to the August skies, and strewn with the litter of the dismantled church, had still a certain mournful dignity, the spirit of Major Cooper, which was the spirit of old Dorset, went into another Present.

THE END.